Wink

by Randie Craft

Book One

Chapter 1

Jace

"Just because *he's* here, you think you're untouchable." The heavyset man's lip curls in defiance, making his sweaty chins wiggle in the dull fluorescent light. "If he wasn't here I would kick your ass up and down this hallway, then send you back to Marty with your tail between your legs." He leans over, ever so carelessly, and spits.

Ty glances down at his once bright white shoes, now speckled with yellow-brown phlegm and chewed tobacco. My pulse quickens at the blatant disrespect. There's no way I'm going to be able to handle this fat fuck's mouth much longer.

Ty slowly lifts his gaze from his ruined shoes, irritation flashing while he visibly fights to keep his temper under control. He flicks his cigarette onto the threadbare carpet. "Ya know, I was going to be nice to you—no really, I was." He shakes his head as he glances back down. "But...do you *know* how much these shoes cost? Not to mention they're a limited-edition, one-time release. They sold out in about three minutes, and

now—no, you look at me. Look at me!" His voice climbs an octave as he finally loses his composure. He nods his head in my direction. I'm slouching up against the crumbling brick wall watching the pointless exchange through narrowed eyes.

"Jace isn't going to touch you. He has a fight tomorrow. It's just you and me tonight, George." Ty straightens and begins folding back the sleeves of his button-up shirt. "And for the record, I don't need him for—"

I push off the wall and clear my throat. "Tyler, you talk too fucking much." This mundane argument might go on forever if I don't cut them off. Three short strides put me face to face with the client. His eyes widen at my approach, but he has nowhere to go in the narrow hallway. His arms visibly pepper with gooseflesh, and his breath quickens.

Weak.

I can't stand weak men.

Most of them don't quiver so much at a simple cocked eyebrow, but then, it's unclear if he could even be called a man. With the way he submits when the local gang bangers walk all over him, it's no wonder he needs Marty's protection. "I don't give a fuck about my fight. I want to get the hell out of this stinking shithole. So you've got about five seconds to fucking pay up before I start pounding every godforsaken dollar you owe Marty out of your pathetic, overweight ass."

"Y-yes, I u-understand. Just wait here, I 'ave some savings in my safe." George edges around me and scurries into his office. An overpowering need to grab him and deliver on my threat pulls me a step toward him. Ty steps in front of me, an expression of displeasure on his face.

"You know the rules, Jace. No fighting during fight camp. I could have handled Mr. Wilam. 'You talk too much, Ty. I don't care about my fight, blah, blah, I'm so tough!'" He mimics me in a horrid rendition of my voice, hands dancing around in the stagnant air. "Piss off, Jace, you fucking caveman." He gives me his favorite three-finger salute.

I can't help but grin at his comment. He's right of course. The rule is "no outside brawling during fight camp," but the dickwad—Marty's "client"—didn't need to know that. I didn't necessarily need to step in either, but I'd been standing there listening to them argue for the better part of ten minutes, and I was bored. In any case, I got the payment process rolling.

Tyler can hold his own well enough. After all, he's one of the people who taught me how to take a punch, though I learned how to give them all on my own. Growing up with him and two other older brothers had its advantages. I can fight in three different styles and adapt to almost any situation. I loved every moment of it, even when I was flat on my back with a broken nose and black eyes, grinning like a madman through crimson teeth. Now, broken noses come few and far between, but I still crave the thrill of a fight. Fighting comes as easily as breathing. The release is euphoric.

When I was a small child I fought my brothers to eat when Mom spent all her money on drugs. I fought kids who made fun of my oversized hand-me-down clothes in school. I even fought the bullies who thought they needed to prey on the weak. Not to save the weak but simply because I wanted to hit someone. I've always enjoyed fighting.

"Just get the money and let's go."

I have no intention of doing Marty's bidding any longer than is fucking necessary. Things have been strained between us for a while now, and I'm not about to start kissing his ass to try to make it better. For the time being, I intend to keep my mouth shut and continue with the same redundant bullshit. I've taken the time to observe the members within the club, figure out who my allies truly are, but my patience is wearing thin, and I'm constantly on edge waiting for someone to see through my facade. I've had to find a balance to avoid losing my shit.

Fighting, sex, and ungodly amounts of Jack Daniels are my coping strategies.

I found that if people stared at me too long it was because they either wanted to fight or fuck. Although, now that I have to keep my record clean, I fight less and fuck more. How I ever made it into my twenties without getting a single charge is beyond me.

Fortunately, booze is constantly available, and there always seems to be enough women—or birds as I like to call them; they're always eager to peck at any attention handed out, no matter how sparse the offerings are. They hang around the clubhouse in small flocks, it annoys me to no end...at least until I have a few shots in me.

"H-here you go. This is all I have." George's eyes seek everything but my own.

As I look inside the small sack it quickly becomes apparent he's short. I close the bag and hand it to Ty. Realizing my body is already set up for the action, I open my hand a bit wider, not wanting to bust my knuckles, and launch it forward. It slams into George's temple, and he falls backward.

"You know, I would say I didn't see that coming, but who the fuck am I joking?"

I shoot a crooked smile at my brother's words as I turn to leave, stepping over the quaking ball of a coward. "Don't blame me. I warned him."

Chapter 2

Lexi

My breath comes in shallow pants. His body quivers under me, but I know better than to underestimate him. I slowly pull my heels together, pushing them into his buckskin ribs. The speed that erupts from him threatens to toss me over the saddle. I extend my legs in the stirrups, taking the pressure off, and his body eases beneath me, although his pace around the pen doesn't slow. It never does, not until I ask for it, which is always where we run into trouble. When I begin to pull back on the bridle, he throws his head side to side, spittle flying everywhere.

"Woah." After adding the verbal command I hunker into my seat, preparing for what is bound to come next.

His hindquarters round under seconds before he thrusts them up in shallow crow-hops. I have no choice but to grab the horn and try to ride through it. Working Trigger always makes me slightly emotional, as it throws my grandfather's death in my face. I envision him standing on the railing telling me to get control of the horse's head. My chest grows tight, making it difficult to breathe. Trigger thrashes out, wanting me off him. He senses my weakness. Three more quick bucks and I'm able to regain control. I turn him in tight circles to the right, straighten and turn to the left, and then dig my heels in again. This time I expect the power and allow him to run until we're both sweating freely and he slows to a canter. I offer a "Woah" as a warning before pulling back on the reins. He comes to a stop, and I quickly dismount. My heart races from the adrenaline and my head is featherlight, but I want to jump up and down with glee regardless. Instead, I choose to calmly pat him on the neck, smiling at our progress.

As I untack him, I realize the sweating might help me shed another few ounces. That will make the weigh-in for my fight this evening easier. Every so often I find myself wondering what it is in my life that draws me to the violence and unpredictability of breaking horses and mixed martial arts.

Is it because I was adopted? Handed off a few months after my birth like I was a puppy the family grew tired of? Or is it because my adoptive parents blinded me with a happy life until I was eight, only to rip the veil away with a hateful, nasty divorce? Maybe this is simply how I would have always dealt with being a normal troubled teen, regardless of the path life took me. Maybe I would still crave the exhilaration of an untamed animal daring me to push the limits. Then again, breaking horses is one thing. To actually physically fight someone is a whole different ball game.

Maybe it's simpler than all that. Maybe it's just who I am. Fighting is in my blood, horse or human. I need that kind of mentally demanding outlet.

A million thoughts race through my mind while I cool down Trigger and put him out to pasture. Today is not the day to be questioning all this. It happens every single damn time though. A faint light illuminates the aging kitchen as I trek back inside. The once sea green cabinets are faded to an almost off white, and peeling along the edges to reveal the raw wood underneath. The hardwood floor is so scuffed in the high traffic area that you cannot see the grain that once told the story of the trees below. A shiver blooms over my body while I wait for the coffee to be brewed. My stomach groans violently as if it, too, is protesting my life choices. The training I put my body through during fight camps is vigorous and not for the faint of heart. The fighting, on the other hand, that's the easy part.

A yawn stretches my face and seizes all thoughts as it brings tears to my eyes. Wiping them away with one hand, I grab two ancient coffee cups with the other. I fill mine only half-way. Black coffee isn't something I'm fond of, but today I can't add creamer or sugar. I need some-thing other than water to sip on though. I pull down two shots of espresso and add them to Ann's coffee, who is sitting facedown at the kitchen table, complaining about being up so early.

"Come on, you know if I didn't have to weigh in this morning I would still be passed out too. I'm no more of a morning person than you are."

Ann leans her head to one side, waving an attenuated arm at me. "Yes, yes, but you and your lovely motivation is sickening. How long has it been since you've eaten, Lex?"

It has been almost forty-eight hours, but I'm not about to tell her that. "I don't know, not that long. I'll be eating here in a few hours."

"You know, come to think of it, I do believe you have become a morning person, dear." I roll my eyes at her flippant subject change. "You wake up before me now, you never did that before we moved here." She sucks in a sharp breath. "It's those 'creatures,' isn't it?"

I laugh at the dramatic way she utters "crea-tures," as if it's the dirtiest word in existence. She means my grandfather's horses and other farm ani-mals.

A small tendril of guilt bubbles in my stom-ach. Today is supposed to be payday. If I had gotten hurt this morning working Trigger, we wouldn't be able to get money to feed the "creatures" or ourselves.

"They do have to be looked after, Ann, and

you won't help with them. Besides, I need to establish a routine before we start school. I have to get up early." I take a tiny sip of my coffee, wincing as the heat and overpowering flavor touches my tongue.

"You're darn tootin' I won't be helping. I need my beauty rest! Also, unlike you, I have all this to tend to." Ann pulls her scrunchie out, and her dark brown locks fall down to her shoulders. "You, on the other hand—well, what exactly do you have to do to get ready? You don't wear makeup. A few swipes of gel and you're peachy. I would kill to look as good as you with short hair." With a flamboyant huff she places her head back on the table, her hair spilling out around her.

"Here, a peace offering." Nudging her gently with my elbow, I offer her the cup that contains espresso loaded with sugar and a splash of milk.

"Oh, sweets. You are my saviour, truly." Snatching the cup away, she takes a long pull. I will never understand how she can taste anything after searing off her taste buds every morning.

"You have no idea how much I appreciate you coming with me today," I remind her.

"Darling, you think too highly of me. It's the half-naked men that draw me to these things." That's only half the truth. Ann has always been there for me. Hell, she moved halfway across the country with me three months ago. California suits her well, though, which I'm thankful for. Not everyone would pick up and leave everything behind like that. "Now, shoo. I'm halfway through my cup of joe, and I want to eat. I'm sorry, but I cannot do it in front of you. I feel you watching me, and it's weird."

"What? I do not watch you." Laughing, I pull on my boots and coat. It's never really cold here, but deep coat pockets make it easier to carry treats for Kashi, my older, gentler horse. Ann rolls her eyes and tilts her cup, draining the remainder of its contents.

I replay the previous day in my head as I walk to the barn, particularly the times Ann has eaten in front of me. Do I really watch her? "I do not... I'm not that weird..." I whisper into the crisp morning air.

Grandpa's farm sits on a remote strip of land, with nearby mountains high enough to block the sunrises that try to peek through each morning. Along the back half of the property, a small but steady river flows just inside the forest line. Sometimes I forget a huge overcrowded city is only an hour away.

The barn is small. It has a few stalls on each side and hasn't been painted since I was young, five maybe. It's my favorite place on the farm, despite its slightly moldy odor. I was thirteen when Mom started sending me here during summertime, after my father stopped asking for me to come visit him. I spent a lot of time in this barn. Grandpa hung a punching bag in the back stall. The busted up bag has witnessed many tear-filled, angry days. It provided an outlet for my unheard screams, and rewarded me in unexpected ways—bloody knuckles and an overall sense of relief. It hasn't moved since Grandpa put it there.

The chicken coop takes up another stall, and a few hens greet me with small clucks and gurgles as they make their way down the ramp. "Talking to myself isn't weird either, huh, ladies?" They look up at me with large unblinking stares, quickly resuming their search for bugs once its clear I have no food for them.

The double doors are already unlatched from the morning workout with Trigger. Kashi watched me sullenly earlier this morning as I pulled the younger horse out and left him. So when I step into his stall he offers me his rump, letting me know how he felt about my sunrise endeavors. The gesture makes me laugh.

"Hey, sweet boy, here ya go." I pull a carrot out of my hoodie, and he quickly changes his attitude, rounding on me with a quiet whinny. "Did you sleep well?" A warm snort between chomps is his answer.

Kashi has been my living diary for as long as I can remember. Grandpa bought him for me during the summer I turned eight, a few months after my parents separated. He was the only good thing to come from their divorce. I trained him during Mom's spontaneous vacations here and eventually every summer too. His presence calms my fraying nerves.

"This girl I'm fighting today... Sh-she's going to be a tough one. She has way more experience than I do..." Kashi finishes his carrot and turns, pushing his head into my hand, ordering me to scratch him. The smell of horse fills my nose, and dirt sifts under my nails as I drag them through his rose-grey coat. I pull a coreless apple from inside my jacket, and he chomps it happily. While he eats his breakfast I wrap my arms around his neck, resting my head. My thoughts again drift to my grandpa and what he might say right now.

"When have you ever balked at something, dangerous girl? She is human, same as you. She has flaws. You just gotta find 'em." His eye would crinkle around the edges as he placed a wad of tobacco in his lip. *"You cannot be afraid to live, Lex my girl, nope, nope. There ain't much to life without living."*

His death nearly broke me. It's taken all my strength not to curl up and forget to live these past six months. It has left me constantly exhausted. My drive to continue is fueled by the fear of disappointing him, regardless that he's gone.

I moved to California a week after I inherited his old farm. The lawyers told me Grandpa had paid for me to go to college at the university in town, and I was eager to be somewhere that filled me with his memory. He knew his passing would affect me deeply and did his damndest to keep me busy through my grief. I will forever be grateful.

Chapter 3

Jace

A few quick raps on my bedroom door pull me from another relentless dream.

"Jace, come on. We have to get going soon."

Every single fucking night the same damned nightmare plagues my mind. My mother, trying to pull me down into the basement as men fill our house searching for my stepfather. Pictures shatter on the hardwood floor with sickening crunches. Mother's beloved china hutch splinters into pieces at the end of a baseball bat. Other things crash behind us as our house is ripped apart during their raid.

"Jace, you up?"

I lie there, chest twisting in pain, staring at my bare wall and trying to regain control over my breathing.

As I drift off again into the weightless place between sleep and consciousness I remember my brothers, Tyler, Scott, and Will, were already down in the darkness hiding... An eerie calm laces my mother's voice, like it's any other day. It sets off pinpricks of panic down my spine. Shadows pass by the door, and the sound of their yelling reverberates in my ears. Then the door creaks open as someone slips down the twisting steps. The shadow grabs me by the throat and squeezes. I hear my mother's sobs and the muffled sound of her punching the shadow. I know I should panic, claw at the hands, but all I can do is focus on the lights swirling behind my eyes as the air is crushed out of me.

When the hand loosens, I fall hard to my knees. Shaky, haggard breaths fill my lungs with a horrible wheezing noise. When the gunshot goes off, wet heat sprays my face. Then I watch, utterly helpless as the cops load Will, my second oldest brother, into a cop car...

I wasn't fully aware of what was happening at the time, but I knew the cops were fucked up, and wherever they were taking him... well, it wasn't to a hospital to help him stop shaking.

Will was only fourteen.

My door slams open and Tyler bounds onto my bed, lying across me with his dead weight.

"Get off, you fuck!" I turn to avoid getting kneed in the nuts, and push my morning wood into naked, soft flesh. The unexpected touch makes me flinch and knock Tyler onto the floor, who nearly takes me with him. He lands with a grunt and begins laughing like an idiot.

"What in the actual fuck! I came in here to tell you coffee is ready, and Cooper wants to know if—" From beside me a body moves under the sheets. As the covers fall away a bushy-haired brunette appears and looks Ty and me over with dull brown eyes.

"I didn't know you were into that sort of thing, Jace, but two Boston brothers sounds better than one." The girl's voice, high and squeaky, has me clenching my jaw. She has to be in her early twenties, and when she blows a kiss at my brother her appeal to me is squished between her fake tits.

Ty stands up, dusting nonexistent dirt from his clothing. I throw my legs off the edge of the bed and push the heels of my palms into my eyes in a final attempt to escape the memories floating within my mind. I refrain from covering my cock as I stand.

"Dude, put that thing away before you poke someone's eye out!" Ty shoves me toward the shower and slaps my ass. As I close the door I hear Tyler suggesting the girl get dressed and leave before I come back.

He has a soft spot for women, and he must think I'll be a dick to her if she sticks around. I, on the other hand, give zero fucks. She knew what she was getting into when she kept bending over directly in front of me to shoot pool last night in the clubhouse. They all know, yet it never stops them. I figure they're trying to fill some void, same as me, but it's the girls who try to get to know me who really make me grind my teeth.

I try to expel all my thoughts in preparation for my fight later. All my training is about to be tested. There's something about fighting that makes me feel...normal. I know I have to be smarter in the upcoming months. I have to rely more on the release fighting in the cage provides, and less on illegal shit.

Chapter 4

Lexi

Butterflies wreak havoc on my stomach as I take in the packed parking lot. Everything inside me is in knots. This show is larger than anything I've ever seen. When I lived in Oklahoma I only fought in amateur events, meaning I didn't get paid. I started looking for a gym to train at before moving here. Fighting is an outlet I happened across by accident, something I fell passionately in love with and was not going to give up easily. I showed up to my first class with the intention of training to go pro. My coach laughed at me. He told me to glove up and that if I didn't go home crying he would consider training me. I left with a black eye, but I was able to begin my training the next day.

I must be broadcasting my thoughts on my face because Ann grabs my hand and squeezes. "Darling, why do you do this to yourself? You always overthink things. I mean, how much harder can this be than your last fight?"

Very. The girl I'm fighting has three other pro fights under her belt, and with each fight comes knowledge. Not wanting to worry her, I shake my head to clear the thoughts. "Yeah, you're right. I just want to get this over with. I'm ready to eat a whole buffalo."

We booked a room in the hotel a few days after getting the okay for my fight, knowing they would likely fill up fast. Even though we're only eighteen, we always manage to con someone at the after parties into buying us drinkage. This way we won't have to worry about paying a taxi to drive us home if we both decide to drink tonight. Most of the time the parties aren't half bad. It depends on how long my fight lasts and how banged up I get if I partake in the festivities or sit on the sidelines smiling while Ann enjoys herself.

"You look amazing by the way." Ann links her arm with mine, and I suddenly grow self-conscious. I'm wearing a short, sleeveless black dress, it makes me look like I'm wrapped in an ACE bandage. The outfit is completed with a pair of high-top converse.

"Thank you," I murmur back. Ann offered to let me wear a pair of her high heels, but I already have two left feet and don't want to trip as I walk on stage.

The weigh-ins are being held in the middle of a grand ballroom where people sit at fancy tables eating fancy foods and drinking fancy foreign beers while they watch the fighters strip down to their undergarments, step on a scale, and face off for promotional propaganda. The only reason I chose to wear a dress was to reduce the time it will take to get undressed, which means less time in front of the hyped-up crowd. I hate being in front of so many people. Every fucking time I feel lightheaded and on the verge of a panic attack. The dress helps speed things up because I only have to slip it off and back on. My converse are already untied and loose as well. Preparation is key.

Standing by the front doors of the hotel are two large men who appear to be working security. I purse my lips. Normally they only take those kinds of precautions at the fights. There is always a handful of people who get a little tipsy and think they're better than the fighters they're watching.

One of the doors swings open, and Nick Norsby, a guy on my team, walks out, a cigarette tucked between his lips. Without looking up he lights it and inhales deeply. In a few long strides I close the distance between us. With one hand I reach out, pluck the cig from his mouth, and flick it into the parking lot.

Nick pulls back from the action. His hands raise automatically, and he shifts his weight into a fighting stance before he recognizes me and relaxes. "Geesus, Lex, it's only you."

"Those things are bad for your health, don't cha know?" I offer him a smile.

"Yeah, well they're not cheap either." He smiles back but refrains from lighting another.

"Why are you so jumpy?"

Nick runs a hand through his dirty-blond hair, then sighs. "Jace Boston is the main event of this fight card."

"Ooh, even that name sounds sexy. Is he? Sexy, I mean?" Ann reaches into her small purse and pulls out her lip gloss, applying another layer over her plump lips.

Nick ignores her. "Every time he's on a fight card all his biker buddies show up and start shit... He's not even *that* good."

"Biker? Like a gang?" Ann asks, purring at his words.

I remember seeing the name on the lineup but have never personally met him before. He trains out of some gym called Valhalla Warriors.

"They don't like to be called that, but pretty much, yeah."

"Well, come on then. What are we waiting out here for? Clearly the party is inside." Ann adjusts herself and nods to the bouncers as she walks in.

I want to follow her, but the butterflies feel like they're crawling up into my throat. "Hey, are you okay?" Nick puts a hand on my shoulder, giving it a gentle squeeze.

Laughing nervously, I slip out of his grip. "Psh, yeah, duh. Why wouldn't I be?"

"No reason. You just look a little pale is all."

"Yeah. Well, cutting weight will do that to ya. You coming?"

Nick looks at the ground, shifting his weight uncomfortably.

He's embarrassed, and I realize he still wants a smoke. "Well, I'll see you inside."

My anxiety sends a prickling sensation to the back of my head as soon as I pass through the glass doors, like a winter breeze is whispering in my ear, breaking my skin out in gooseflesh. The room is filled with people. Most of them are seated at round tables throughout the room. Others stand talking along the sides or at the bar nestled at the back of the large space.

An idea flicks across my brain—a crazy, dumb idea—but if I want it to work I have to hurry. I scan the crowd and see Ann chatting up a few guys; she didn't notice my entrance. Putting on my brave face I walk toward the back of the room, keeping my head low.

The bar is super crowded, and the server bounces from customer to customer while twirling bottles and pouring various liquids. Leaning in between two people I call out, "A shot of Disaronno, please." I hold out the money, taking advantage of having a person on either side of me. As a fighter, I have no idea what kind of trouble I would get in drinking the day of my fight and being underage, and I'd rather not find out. For a moment I think it will work, but as the bartender takes the money he looks me over, narrowing his eyes.

"You twenty-one, kid?"

I try to scoff. "I am not a kid..." *Say something else... Say something before he tells you to get lost!* I stare at the barkeep for what feels like an eternity, until a voice that sounds like smoke and whisky pulls me from my panic.

"Hey, Thomas, don't be a tight-ass. She's with me. Put it on my tab."

My left eye begins to twitch from the strain of not turning around to see who saved my ass. I try to act casual, although I know I must look like I'm having a seizure. The server's eyes seem to glaze over as he pulls a shot glass from under the counter, quickly filling it to the brim with my favorite amaretto flavored liqueur. Without a second glance, he slides it across the bar, along with my money. I purse my lips. It must be nice to have a tab.

I slam the drink back before he can ask any more questions and before anyone recognizes me, then turn to leave, all the while praying that the man who bought me the drink—who obviously must think I'm someone else—will apologize and let me go on my way. But I'm not that lucky. In my haste to leave I manage to trip over my untied shoelaces and stumble right into the man's well-defined chest.

The guy is wearing a white T-shirt and faded blue jeans. He wraps a large hand around my elbow and holds me steady as I try to regain my composure. Heat rises to the tips of my ears. Pulling away, I tilt my head up to offer a sincere apology, but his hazel eyes beg my undivided attention, causing my words to tangle in my throat. All I manage to say is, "Yourfrum."

What the hell!?

The man laughs, and my eyes lower to his succulent lips. "Fucking lightweights." While his words seem like an insult, his eyes hold a playful glint. They're beautiful. The color reminds me of honey with rays of sun passing through the amber liquid. His nose looks like it's been broken multiple times, but this feature only adds points to my mental calculation of how handsome he is. His body is as rigid as his jawline, and there are tattoos tracing around his forearm up to his bicep. I give myself a mental shake, which is exactly what I needed to pull me out of my stupor—that or the heat blooming in my belly has finally relaxed me enough to think clearly.

"Excuse me. If you could move out of my way, that would be great." My irritation at my own behavior laces my words with a bite not intended for him, causing me to wince.

One of his thick brows rises. "What, not even going to thank me?"

Something strange stirs inside me. His thick voice calms me, like we're old friends. I want to ask him his name. I want to pull him into the locker room to see where else he has tattoos. My stomach clenches at the heated thoughts, and I look away.

I see Nick walking through the crowd, heading straight for us, and my heart drops. "Thank you. Now, if you'll excuse me, my boyfriend is waiting for me," I lie, hoping I can get away without being busted.

He nods slightly, stepping aside. I release the breath I didn't realize I was holding. When I walk past, his hand slips around my wrist with a gentle but firm hold. The warmth that radiates from the touch makes me break out in a cold sweat. I know I'm running the risk of him finding out he just bought a minor a drink, yet I don't instantly pull away. Instead, I meet his eyes with a questioning look.

"I never got your name."

Lie. Don't tell him your real name.

"It's Lexi." *That was not lying, you moron!*

"Well it's nice to meet you, Lexi. I hope I didn't piss your boyfriend off too badly." His eyes look past me, and I know it must be Nick he's referring to. A cold sensation prickles down my spine.

"He'll get over it," I say and pull away. His hand glides over mine, his fingertips brushing against my sweaty palm. Dragging my eyes from his ruggedly handsome face, I walk away with a slight smile and no remaining trace of panic or anxiety.

Nick has a hard set to his jaw. I briefly wonder if I actually did piss him off somehow. But when I reach him he appears more concerned than anything. "You okay?" he asks for the second time today, glancing from me to the man I left behind.

"Yeah, I just got turned around. He, uh, that guy was telling me where the locker rooms were at," I say, pulling Nick in that direction, even though I already know where they are.

He shakes his head and laughs like he heard something unbelievable.

"What?" My heart flutters nervously as I wonder if he saw me taking that shot. I have plenty of time for my buzz to wear off before my fight tonight, so it isn't that big of a deal. Although, me being underage is kind of an issue.

"Man, he's such a dick. He could have just taken you to them. It's exactly like I was telling you."

"What are you talking about?"

"That's Jace Boston...the main event for tonight. The guy who's"—Nick's voice drops an octave—"in the biker gang."

Oh, shit—not good.

I spare a quick glance over my shoulder to see Jace still at the counter. A few people are talking to him, but his eyes are on me. He winks, and my entire body jolts forward. I duck my head and all but drag Nick backstage.

Chapter 5

Jace

For as long as I can remember I've always been able to read people well. I can tell when they're lying or if, in general, they're simply stupid fucks. So I know the girl was lying about having a boyfriend, although I don't know why. She's attracted to me, that's obvious, even if she wasn't broadcasting it like most birds. She actually sounded annoyed with me, and I have to admit is kinda hot.

Although, maybe I have it wrong, because she walked right into the arms of Nick Norsby, who totally had a pissed-off-boyfriend look on his face. When she glanced back I couldn't help but send her a wink. She's shorter than I prefer my birds but has all the right curves, her little dress flaunts them nicely. I briefly wonder what she would be like in bed, and as I imagine her plump lips wrapped around my cock, I get the feeling I've seen her before. She has a distinctive exotic look, with those large blue eyes and equally large ears that she tries to hide by spiking out her short blonde hair.

It bothers me that I can't place her. Remembering people is what I do. My thoughts are interrupted by a loud "Welcome, ladies and gentlemen! It's time to start what you have all been waiting for...the face-offs!" A thundering roar erupts from the crowd. Here and there a shrill whistle fills the air. I push my way past the small group that has been trying to get me to sign various memorabilia, and I make my way to the locker rooms. Face-offs are a vital part of my game plan. A single stare can fuck with my opponent's mind and win me the fight.

As I walk, I pop in my earbuds and take out my phone to pull up my playlist. Time to go take a nap before I'm needed on stage. Tyler will find me when it's my turn...which is very fucking last. No reason to have to listen to the coaches nagging their fighters about how much they weigh and asking if they need to take a quick piss or shit to shed a few extra ounces. I hate hearing fighters bitch and moan because they're not mentally strong enough to cut weight on their own. I'm super strict during my fight camps, so my weight is never an issue.

Leaning my head against the wall, my eyelids droop as the soothing beats of Dubstep begin to echo in my ears.

Sometime later a tap on my shoulder interrupts my blissfully blank mind. Ty gestures for me to take my earbuds out. "It had better be time to get naked," I snap.

"Why the fuck you always so eager to show people your junk?"

"Why you so afraid of showing people yours? You worried the girls will laugh?"

"More like run away in fear."

"You call it 'little button,' don't you?"

Tyler throws an empty water bottle at me. "And you say I talk too much. Come on, you're up next—the females are weighing in now."

Shoving my phone back into my pocket, I follow Ty to the side of the stage where I'm supposed to come out. Fighters for each match come out on opposite sides of the platform. The girl beside me is standing off to the side of the stage, waiting for them to call her up. She trains with one of our affiliate gyms. Tough chick, but she lacks commitment and heart. Not super attractive either. I recall her opponent's stats. Her name is Alexis Trucco. She's five foot three inches, and this is her debut pro fight. She hasn't been in a lot of amateur fights but has a decent record. Everyone loves watching females go at it, resulting in them getting paid a hefty amount.

The announcer's voice blasts out of the speakers next to me, making my ears ring: "First, we have our local fighter, fighting out of Punishment MMA! I give you Linda 'The Snake Bite' Sissom!" Linda walks out in a jogging suit, dark hair piled on top of her head. She shimmies out of her pants and top, revealing only a strapless bra and matching undies. She has a nice body; I'll give her that, though a bit thin for my taste. "One hundred thirty-two pounds, five ounces." She walks to the middle of the stage. "Her contender, fighting out of American Elite, Alexis 'The Beautiful Disaster' Truccoooooooooo!"

As the opposing girl steps onstage, my lips part. It's the girl from the bar. A grin splits my face as the announcer calls out her stats. *You fucking idiot, you bought a minor a drink.* This is a twenty-one-and-over event. It didn't even cross my mind that she could be underage. The little broken law doesn't hold my attention long. This chick is smoking hot, and now that I know she's a fighter, she's even more attractive. Nick must be one of her teammates.

She drops her dress to her ankles, which only adds to my mental image of her naked. "One hundred thirty-five pounds on the mark!" She's shorter than her opponent, putting her at a disadvantage, but—

Damn, her thick legs and ass... She has the perfect body. Flat stomach revealing a toned four pack. Nicely defined arms. Looks like she might have some power.

"Jace, you ready?" Ty's voice interrupts my thoughts. *Thanks, cock block...*

I pull off my hoodie. "Yup, let's get this shit over with."

∞∞∞

Lounging in a hotel all day is one of the best things about fighting. Marty won't call me tonight. I get to escape it all for a little while. Sprawled out across the king-size bed, my thoughts drift back to the female fighter from the weigh-ins. Alexis Trucco. I can't believe I failed to realize who she was. I saw her face at least a dozen times when I checked the fight card, making sure nothing had changed. She's cute. Seeing her trip over her own feet and fall into Nick's arms caused a surge of jealousy, an emotion I'm not familiar with. I have a different woman every night. What is there to be jealous about?

This chick will turn out to be like all the rest, spreading her legs to anyone who can give her what she's looking for. I don't understand why I'm even still thinking about her. My fight is only a few hours away. I need to relax and not think about some bird I don't even know and likely never will.

Chapter 6

Lexi

No matter how many times I use the rest-room I still have the sensation that I need to pee. It annoys me to the point that I can't focus on the fight before mine. The waiting part is always the hardest. This fight could end any second, and I'll be up. Or it could go all three rounds and I'll be waiting for fifteen minutes. My stomach begins to roll, and I think I need to use the restroom again, but I know this urge won't go away until I hear the clank of metal on metal—the sound the cage doors make when fighters got locked inside.

When I hear that beautiful sound, my instincts take over, and all my fear, my thoughts of being inadequate, disappear. That's when I get to work out my issues. I get to breathe out the strange anger that swirls inside me, the things that make me the fucked-up individual I am. The abandonment issues, I got when my adoptive father turned his back on Mom and me. My issues with authority, I have because my mom was more concerned with being my friend than my mother. Or my general distrust of men, which I have because through the years they seemed to have more pull over my mother's decisions than I did. I could blame my parents, the ones who adopted me, the ones who raised me, but that would be unfair. They saved my life—even my father, regardless of his failure at being a decent role model.

If you really look at my life you'll see that most likely my mental issues come from the part of my life before they adopted me. My biological mother was an alcoholic and on various illicit drugs. I remember nothing from that age. My adoption was finalized on my first birthday. If the reports are to be believed, I was neglected from birth and until Marie and Paul saved me.

I was born premature and had underdeveloped lungs. I have a small ugly scar across my stomach—it looks like something extremely hot rolled across the tender skin—and various other faded burns that resemble cigarette marks. I had a rash so bad I couldn't even wear a diaper without screaming in pain because my own urine burned it. Marie let me run around naked peeing on everything so I wouldn't be in constant agony. My teeth had to be capped in silver because the only thing my egg donor gave me to drink was the free juice from the WIC office.

Some distant relatives came to see me when

I was about sixteen and told me how happy they were I had been adopted. They went on to tell me about a time they came over when my biological mother still had me. They said I never cried. I would lie flat on my stomach, unmoving, when she snapped her fingers.

I felt like I was hearing about some other child, that all those terrible things couldn't have happened to me. I can't remember any of it. I feel empty inside when anyone brings up my life from before. I mean, if this is what people saw and reported...what happened when no one was looking?

All the awesome things babies get to experience, I missed out on. Until Marie and Paul made me apart of their family. They spoiled me with love and affection but I still felt something was missing. Until I found punching things released something within me. I came into the world fighting and to this day it's the thing I do best.

When I step into the cage, it's only me and my opponent. I stop thinking about every little thing I do or analyzing everything I say over and over until it becomes meaningless. Something deep inside my subconscious takes over, and I'm free. I feel normal. No more pretending I'm someone I'm not. My fist impacting someone's face makes me smile. I can be the monster I truly am, disguised by a sweet smile and cowgirl boots.

Loud cheering and shrieks pull me from my thoughts. The match is over. My fight is next. I walk to the stage entrance, still hidden from the looming crowd. Panic prickles the back of my skull. Every time I fight, it's at this moment I want to run. I'm knowingly putting myself in danger, and everything inside me screams, "This is crazy!"

An overbearing voice announces my name on the speakers, and then my walk-out song, "Run This Town" by Rihanna, comes on, blasting throughout the entire room. My face twitches into a smile as the words speak to my soul.

I step out from the shadows, revealing myself to the thrill-seeking crowd. Everything around me fades away, and the lyrics flow through me. When I reach the steps that lead to the cage, a hand grabs my shoulder, pulling me from my trance. Nick stands behind me, a serious look in his emerald eyes. He smears Vaseline across my cheeks, nose, and eyebrows. His mouth is moving, but the words drift away in the stale air. He hugs me, and I turn around, lifting my legs one by one up the steps. The cool vinyl of the cage floor kisses my feet.

I go directly to my corner and bounce around to stay moving. Linda's name is announced, and her song blares over the speakers. She receives Vaseline and words of encouragement from her cornerman, then enters. Again my face splits into a grin. I'm not doing it to intimidate her but because I know in a few meager seconds my panic, my fear, everything will disappear.

The euphoric ping of the metal lock clicks

my brain into hyperawareness. The noise of the crowd rushes in like someone cranked up the volume of a radio. A thick coppery smell assaults my nose. The movements of my opponent draw my gaze as we await the bell that tells us to begin. The referee asks us if we're both ready. I nod, eager to test my skills. The ref raises his hand and at Linda's nod drops it.

The fight has begun.

She rushes me, throwing a flurry of straight punches. I cover up, stepping back and trying to watch her movements. She drops her hands for a split second before throwing her power hand. That's when I see my opening. I step forward, twist my hips, and connect a right hook to her face, stunning her. I follow up with a left cross, a right jab, a left hook. Then, to create space, I end it with a right body kick. She staggers back, dazed. I smile, and the fire in her eyes fades. She underestimated me, which pisses me off. Time to have fun!

My chest feels like it's being split in two. My lungs are on fire. My energy is slipping from my body. My mind begs me to stop. If we give up now it will end. The pain will ease and we can rest.

I want to listen.

I almost do.

Linda's peppering punches bring sweltering tears to my eyes. Each strike wears me down as I stumble around the cage. Staggering, I drop to a knee, and Linda shoots in, capitalizing on my weakness. Her weight pushes into me, and she wraps her arms around my neck. Within seconds two different options flash behind my eyes. I could stay crumpled on the mats and allow Linda to sink her arm in deeper across my throat, squeeze, and put me to sleep, resulting in her win. Or...I could tuck my chin and do what ever the fuck I need to do to get the hell out of this dangerous position.

I'm not able to make a conscious decision before my body begins reacting. My hips arch out, heels digging into the mat, and my hands scramble to find an anchor point on her arm. Using all my remaining strength I create the millimeters of space needed for my breath and blood flow to continue. Linda's arms tremble as they squeeze around me. Just as my vision begins to fade I attempt, one last time, to break free.

I can't even tell you exactly how I manage to escape, but as I pull myself to my feet the bell rings, signaling the end of the fight.

Chapter 7

Jace

I have this love-hate relationship with female fights. Chicks are generally better than dudes. While I think they should have been accepted into MMA to fight long ago, I do think they get too much hype. Women should have never been put into these fragile little boxes and pampered like delicate flowers. However, this fight totally deserves credit. It's keeping my attention. My eyes follow the girls back and forth as they trade punches. Alexis has a solid jab and a gnarly right hook, but she lacks experience on the ground. Linda tries submitting her a few times but, despite her inexperience, Alexis is able to maneuver out of each hold and brings the fight back to standing. Linda's experience is put to the test by Alexis's heart. All too soon the ref is holding each girl by the wrist, about to declare the winner.

"Split decision! The winner is...Linda SIS-SOMMMM!"

That was a tough match to judge, which is why you never let it go to the judges. Finish that shit or don't bitch when you lose.

Then Nick enters the cage and wraps an arm around Alexis.

Fucking bastard.

Alexis holds her head high and congratulates her opponent with a genuine smile.

My fight is up now, and my shot of winning Fight of the Night is out the window. Fucking vaginas always win the awards. Might as well go for Knockout of the Night, it actually sounds like a great idea at this point. I'm ready for this night to be over.

When I reach the cage my opponent is already waiting. The doors lock, and the ref asks if we're ready. For a full round I bait my opponent, drawing him in with a dropped hand and lighting him up when he steps into my striking zone. His eye is bleeding, and I know I have to finish this as soon as the second round begins. If his eye starts bleeding again they could stop the match.

Tyler hands me a bottle of water, not saying anything. He knows I'm not listening anyway. I take a swig and spit it out. The bell rings, and I take three strides forward. Panicked, the guy throws a sloppy jab. I easily sidestep, cutting forward so I'm looking at the side of his face. I throw a cross to his jaw, and even before he hits the ground I'm walking away. Hands raised, I search the crowd for my bird of the night. That knock-out should make things easy.

∞∞∞

Red and blue lights flash in the darkness, and I watch my brother's confused face as he is handcuffed and loaded into the back of a cruiser. Then I go back inside to Mom cooking dinner like nothing completely fucked up just happened. A strange discomfort hits me when I look in the mirror— seeing someone else's blood all over my face, feeling the stickiness of it. I'm not sure why, but it affects me more than actually seeing the lifeless body as the cops dragged us from the basement.

A heaviness presses on my chest, and an unpleasant pressure drags me from the darkness. Blinking, I lift my head to find some blonde chick clinging to my chest. Sighing heavily, I push her to the side. I hate it when they invade my personal space.

Wide awake with Will's face swirling in my mind, I throw my legs over the edge of the bed and stand. Rubbing my face vigorously, I try to shake the sensation of damp blood clinging to my skin. Nothing but slight stubble greets my open palm. Still, the desire to wash and scrub my entire body pulls me to the bathroom.

The hot steam hits my body, causing different muscles to tense, then relax slowly. My mind works over various thoughts, and one keeps drawing my attention. It's been too long since I've been to visit Will. Maybe I can tell him about my impending deployment… I know I can't, but the idea of talking to someone about it is tempting.

As I turn off the shower and begin to towel off I can hear the bird in my room getting dressed. I take my time cleaning my ears and teeth. When I get to my room the girl is sitting on my bed looking a bit pissed.

"Good morning," I say as I walk to my dresser.

"Why do you have to be like that?" The blonde crosses her arms and pushes her bottom lip out slightly. A trait that stops me in my tracks.

"Savanna, what the fuck? How in the hell did I end up with you last night?" I throw off my towel and yank open my dresser drawers.

"Real nice, Jace." She bends over, slipping her foot back into her knee-high leather boots. "Real fucking gentlemenlike."

"You know better than to expect that shit from me. What happened last night anyway?" I still have the taste of Jack Daniels in my mouth after brushing my teeth. It's a drink that doesn't always bring out my best side.

"You and Marty got into an argument at the after-party. Said you shouldn't have knocked the guy out like that."

That sounds like something Marty would say, fucking bastard. He's the president of the club, and my mother's old man. He's not my biological father but still takes it upon himself to open his fucking mouth like he is. If I'm being honest, I looked up to the man for most of my childhood, telling everyone he was my father, until the night he left us all to fend for ourselves after a gun deal went sour. The night Will got put away for life.

I have a splitting headache and want this conversation to end. "Listen, sounds to me like both of us made some bad choices last night. Can we just get this over with without all the bull-shit?"

Standing, she starts for the door, then stops. "You know, one day you're going to end up alone. You push everyone who tries to love you away."

I can't help but laugh. "Oh, really, that's what this is? You trying to love me? Listen, the sooner I'm alone, the better. If you don't want to get hurt, I suggest you remember that the next time you think I'm all vulnerable and shit."

After Savanna leaves, I pull on my jeans and lace up my Doc Martens. Pulling my shirt over my head, I move into the living room, where Ty and Cooper sit playing video games. Coop might as well be a Boston brother too. He and I have been friends for as long as I can remember.

Ty glances over and smiles. "Dude, you fucked up bringing her home again."

"No one fucking asked you, dick lips."

Ty throws his hands up. "Woah, no reason to get all hostile, little brother. All I'm saying is—"

"Breakfast is ready!" Diah's voice cuts into

our bickering, and the need to fill my stomach with something other than alcohol takes over. Cooper has been dating this girl for a few months now. It doesn't seem super serious, but she's an alright chick. She can hold her own around us, that's for sure. Plus, she's an amazing cook. Coop wraps his arms around her and starts kissing her.

Tyler starts pretend gagging. "Get a room!" he hoots at them.

"Shut up. You seriously need to get laid, man," Cooper shoots back.

"Hey, I'm not like you two and just give the goods to whoever will jump on them—no offense, Diah."

Diah starts handing out plates. I take mine with a thanks, and as she goes to give Tyler his she drops it. Glass shatters on the ground.

"Tyler, what the hell, man?" Cooper shakes his head as he takes a seat at the bar next to me.

"Yeah, Ty, you better clean that up before someone gets hurt," I add in.

Tyler's eyes widen, bouncing between the three of us.

"You have the grip of an old lady—no offense, Tyler," Diah says as she sits down to eat. We all burst out laughing.

My phone vibrates, and I pull it out, seeing Marty's name flash across the top with a message saying, "*Elliot's Pawn Shop.*

"All right, come on, we have some business to attend to this morning." I shove my phone back in my pocket, take a few more bites, and push a frustrated Ty out the door.

Chapter 8

Lexi

Sitting in Grandpa's old rusted pickup truck, I try to mentally prepare myself for the day. Ann and I are sitting in the campus parking lot about to head to a mandatory orientation for freshmen. Shortly before he died my grandfather had a fund set up in my name that I could only use for schooling purposes, so I've decided to put it to use. For now I'm stuck with the core curriculum, but ultimately I'm going for creative writing. I've always had a passion for the arts. I've bounced around between photography, drawing, and painting, but my passion truly lies with literature. I have no idea what I'm going to do with my degree once I get it, but I'll figure that out in time.

The thought of going to this big-city school without Ann is terrifying. High school was bad enough even when she was there to support me. Ann has been my best friend since we were in sixth grade. I have no idea what I would do without her.

We're polar opposites. While I worry about saying the wrong thing, she says exactly what she's thinking, without the usual mind-to-mouth filter. Despite my tough-girl look, I'm never happy with myself. She's comfortable in her own skin, fearless. While I most often keep to myself, she's wide open. I always feel out of place, and I'm afraid of quite a few things, but that, too, I mostly keep to myself, except when I'm talking with Ann.

So I made a deal with her. She'll come to college with me, and I will loan her the money for tuition. Then she can pay me back after we get real jobs. She wants to become a fashion artist, so she's getting an associate's in commercial arts. The money I got from my fight with Linda will cover her first semester, so I need to be back in the cage by winter. That thought reminds me of the shiner I got a few nights ago. It's faded to an ugly gray purple, and I'm tempted to cover it with makeup, but honestly, I'm simply too tired to care. I only hope it won't put me in a counselor's chair straight out of the gate.

"Holy makerolie, Lex, look!" I follow her dramatic pointing and waving to a gaggle of real-life Barbie dolls—dipped in designer clothes, sprinkled with bleach-blonde hair, and topped off with fake boobs and unnaturally orange complexions.

California's style doesn't appeal to me. The people here are wildly different from back home. At Grandpa's ranch, it is easy to forget where we are, forget how out of place I'm going to be in school. I click my dusty cowgirl boots together and sigh, knowing where this conversation is headed.

"We must go shopping, love! You are in dire need of a wardrobe update, and I need to make a good first impression in my field of education."

"Um, no, we have to go to orientation. We can't skip it." People's first impressions of me are all pretty much the same.

Troubled youth.

I have tattoos, a lip piercing, and short hair. Add in my don't-give-a-shit attitude and bingo, you get a label.

"Um, yes! Orientation is what, an hour, maybe two? That leaves a gazillion hours to shop!"

Finally working up enough courage to leave the old Ford Courier, which is surrounded by Mustangs and Bentleys, we cross the campus and work our way toward the main building. I hear someone call my name and turn to see Nick jogging up to us.

"Hey, I didn't know you went to school here." He tucks a cigarette behind one ear.

"Yeah, today is our orientation. We start later this week. What about you?"

"Lexi, I'll wait for you inside." Ann waves to Nick, then disappears behind two large, ominous doors. My nerves begin to turn icy, and my breath becomes shallow as I realize I will be entering the building alone.

"I have two years left to get my bachelor's in

physical therapy. Hey, have you joined any clubs yet?"

"Clubs? Like chess club?" My brain is foggy, but the conversation is light and distracts me from my panic.

Nick's laugh is nice to hear. I can't help but think of how attractive he is. He has a short, athletic build, still taller than me but not by much. He's what you'd call a pretty boy. From what he's told me he was a bit chunky as a kid. He lost the weight when he found mixed martial arts and says being heavier humbled him. "No, like the Brazilian jiu-jitsu club they just started a few months ago. It's not bad, a great building block for your MMA."

From what I know about Brazilian jiu-jitsu, it's simply groundwork. I prefer to stand up and trade punches. My whole ground game involves working my way to standing back up. "I don't know. I don't think it would really be my thing."

"You never know unless you try. How about this, you come down to Bones tonight. We can play a game of darts, and if you lose, you have to come to one class with me."

Bones is the club where Nick works as a bartender. We've gone a few times already. It's a nice place, other than the fact that they make underage customers wear bright neon wristbands like crime scene tape so no one will offer them alcohol. "And if you lose?"

"Loser buys dinner?"

I click my mouth shut and smile; I've always loved a challenge. "Wait, so if I lose I have to go to this class *and* buy you dinner? That doesn't sound fair."

"I mean, that sounds fine to me." Nick laughs again, and I cannot help but smile.

I sigh. "Sure, what time?"

"My shift is over at ten. Want to meet then?"

Realization hits me, and I fumble with my words. "Sure, Ann wants to go shopping after our orientation. Then *we* can meet you there tonight." I'm not mentally prepared to take on a relationship, and Nick is too good of a friend to simply have a fling with, no matter how tempting it sounds. Seeing the quick flash of hurt doesn't help the situation.

He recovers quickly and says, "Sounds good. See you later."

"Laters," I say, ducking around him and rushing in to find Ann.

Orientation ends with me scolding myself for being worried about nothing. The professor talked about basic stuff, explained various aspects of the school, handed out our student IDs, and sent us on our way. No one so much as gave me a second glance, even with my black eye.

Shopping, on the other hand, is a total disaster. Ann dissects Nick's offer for dinner and somehow has me actually contemplating my stance with him. We get a few outfits, have dinner, and go home to get ready.

"Listen, all I'm saying is, he's clearly interested, and you have needs." Ann dabs on some lip gloss as I sit on the bathroom counter swinging my feet over the edge.

My mind brings up an image of Nick at practice, all sweaty, with his blond hair clinging to his forehead, sweat dripping from the tips. Imagining what it would be like to have his hands on me makes my lower stomach clench, until the face in my daydream shifts to that of Jace Boston, smiling confidently as I push him backward and climb on top of him. Shaking my head, I run a frustrated hand down my face and sigh. "Yeah, it's been a while."

"So it's settled. Tonight you're getting laid!"

Chapter 9

Jace

I can't admit to anyone how much I've grown to loathe the club, how I think the direction in which it's going is destined to either kill us all or put us in prison for life. I can't admit it, and I feel like my window to escape is closing rapidly. Yet I play along with their game like nothing is amiss.

When Marty pulls Ty and me aside to talk to us about new business, I work to keep the hatred for the man from showing in my eyes.

"I don't understand what the issue is, Tyler. All you two fuck nuts have to do is show your faces at the joint." He leans back in the chair at the head of the table.

Tyler interlaces his fingers and leans forward. "This is not how we handle things. This is too public."

Marty stands up, rounding his knuckles on the table between us. "If you want to hold this seat one day you had better man the fuck up. People need to see your face; they need to fear you just as much as they do your enforcers. You must show control over your members, over your business partners."

I stand up and turn to leave before my facade can slip from my fingertips.

"Where the fuck are you going?" The old man growls at me, and my stomach turns to ice.

Over the years, my respect for the man I once considered my father has turned into resentment. It's not about the way he treats my mother —she treats him just as badly. It's not even the beatings he has dealt me over the years. No, it all stems from his inability to protect his own. To protect my brother, Will.

"Do you want this done or not?" I say over my shoulder as I open the door and walk out, not looking back at the pissed-off look I know must be plastered across the bastard's face.

The ride over to the prospective business establishment is quiet. I'm becoming uneasy with how little Ty said.

"He's going to make you pay for walking out like that."

That's more fucking like it. "Let him try."

Tyler pulls into the parking lot and kills the engine. "One day your 'no one can touch me' attitude is going to get you killed."

"One day your 'follow the leader' attitude is going to get *you* killed."

His grip tightens on the steering wheel, and I know I've struck a chord. He should know better than to play mind games with me. I have a bad habit of dealing low blows without a second thought. Dropping his hands, he sighs. "Let's just get this over with." As we get out of the car, he shakes his head at the neon sign before us. "Bones. What a brilliantly clever club name."

I smile and clap him on the shoulder. "Lets go get drunk."

The air inside is thick with sweat as we push our way to the bar. Twenty minutes later I have enough shots in me that my head has stopped overanalyzing everything. Tyler gets himself involved in a hand of poker, and I make my way to the restroom. The crowd on the dance floor begins to thin as I reach a lounge area. A voice pulls my attention to a dartboard off to the side.

"You're cheating; you're totally cheating!" A female with a nice rounded ass dressed in tight blue jeans stands before the board. My eyes work their way up to a black tank top and a short haircut that instantly summons memories of Alexis Trucco. Something catches her attention, and she turns her head. My assumption is confirmed. My eyes zero in on Nick Norsby, who's saying something to her that I can't hear. She laughs and punches him in the arm.

I change directions and head straight for her. She walks away from Nick as he turns to face the dartboard, a few darts in his grip. She stops at a table with a couple of people I don't know, picks up a drink, and takes a sip.

"You con some lucky guy here to buy your drinks for you?" She almost spits out her drink as she looks up at me.

The word "shit" slips from her mouth as she regains composure. I lean in closer to her.

"It's okay. Your secret is safe with me." One of the girls at the table eyes me, then shoots Alexis a questioning look. I catch a heated glare from Nick before he walks up.

"Lexi, it's your turn."

She takes a long pull from her drink. Realizing she does have something extra inside her cup, I wink at her knowingly.

"Okay," she says and walks away quickly.

I grin like a fool and head off to relieve myself.

Exiting the restroom, I see Alexis leaning against the wall, arms crossed. When she sees me she pushes off and strides up to me, all business.

"Listen, no one knows about me drinking before weigh-ins the other day. I would like to keep it that way, okay?"

"What makes you think I care enough to tell them?" *Dude, you're really pulling out the dick card this early? Oh well, can't take it back now.*

She pauses briefly. "Right, well just if you had the idea to say something—don't." She turns to leave.

"Your friends don't know you drink? Do

they think you're some fucking innocent little girl?"

She rounds on me, her face only inches from mine, and the sweet smell of Disaronno greets my nose. "You don't care, remember? So don't ask questions like you do—and I am *not* a little girl."

Damn, she's in a mood. "I feel like we should get to know each other better before you start giving it to me like that." As another person starts down the narrow hallway toward the restroom, I push my way forward, pinning her to the wall without actually touching her. Her breathing picks up, and my eyes lock onto her lips, then flick up to her eyes. I pull back from the fierce look within them. Placing my hand on the wall beside her head, I lean in close to her ear. "You had better go back to your boyfriend before we have another secret to keep from him."

She lingers, and her eyes drop to my lips. I lick them for good measure. "He's not my boyfriend." She reaches up. For a split second I think she's going to slap me, but her hand curls behind my neck and our lips collide. Without a second thought my lips part, and her warm tongue traces circles on mine. My hips respond instinctively and push into hers. Her body answers mine, and she leans into me. My growing erection pushes into her stomach due to our height difference, and she moans. Her hot breath kisses my ear. My arms break out in gooseflesh, and I wrap an arm around her hips, lifting her up. Her toes are barely touching the ground as I lower my face to her neck. Then her hands are on my chest, groping at first, then pushing me away. We come apart, breathing heavily. Her body trembles as my hands fall to my sides. Her eyes pull emotions from me like a black hole, and I have to blink rapidly to stop myself from diving into them again. She drops her gaze, a small blush rising on her cheeks, and pushes past me, leaving me to adjust myself before I follow her.

I search the lounge, only to find her pulling her female friend out onto the dance floor. Nick eyes me briefly before heading after her. Fuck, I need a few more drinks before I can do this without knocking his ass out. I head off to the bar before I change my mind. The thought of punching him is way too tempting.

I find Tyler with a royal flush at the poker table. From the sound of all the jeers he's receiving, he's been hustling them. When I sit down I instantly know things are tense between the players. From the raised platform where we're sitting I can see out onto the dance floor, and it takes no time at all for my eyes to find Alexis with her friend, dancing like her sanity depended on it. My eyes drink her movements in, and the conversation around me blurs. Her hips sway and her breasts bounce with each dip. She raises her hands above her head, revealing a small section of the skin above her pelvis. The whisky in my mouth turns sour as Nick steps up behind her, placing his hands on her body. Instantly the noise around me rushes back in, and Tyler's agitated voice assaults my ears.

"If you weren't so incompetent maybe you would have had better luck. Although, I do doubt it very much." His words slur, and only seconds slip by before I pick up on the hostility pouring from him. The man he's talking to stands up. Taking the movement as a threat, I follow suit. Tyler is on his feet and diving into the dude before I have time to make any sort of judgement. Then someone tries to reach for Tyler, and I instantly jump in. This effectively dictates the direction in which this evening will be headed.

Chapter 10

Lexi

His hands are on me, slipping under my shirt while he pushes me against the wall with a deranged passion. His lips are hot on my skin, leaving scorching trails as he works his way down my neck. His manhood presses into my stomach, sending electricity coursing through my veins. Then I shove him away, and he stumbles back. Looking around, I realize we're locked in an MMA cage, gloves covering our hands. He raises his fists. Briefly, shock stuns my mind, but then men rush past me toward him, and I realize his fists were never meant for me. Dozens of men rush him, and he falls away into the crowd.

I jerk upright in bed. My breath catches in my throat, I blink away the images and pull in deep lungfuls of air as I realize it was only a dream. Well, sort of.

I know I won't get back to sleep, so I get dressed and head down to the stables. Flipping on the barn lights, I give Kashi his morning treats and head for the next stall. Kashi nickers when I don't bestow him with the attention I usually give. Trigger dances anxiously within his stall. He's about three years old—the son of my mother's horse, Kitty, the old mare who's now living the good life out in the pasture. Grandpa laid the groundwork with him; he can be haltered, led, and even lunged. In fact, he worked with Trigger routinely until the day he passed away, and his absence seemed to have affected the young horse. He's flighty and skittish. I know I have my work cut out for me to fully gain his trust, but I'm enjoying the challenge.

I find a calming peace when I work with him. Unlatching his stall and stepping in, I push all thoughts from my mind. Breaking a horse reminds me a lot of fighting; it's a mental game.

In the round pen it all starts well. Trigger is eager, and I'm determined. Then memories of the night at the club slip into my mind—the kiss in the hallway, if you could even call it that. Am I really so desperate that I'm willing to jump any man who pays me the slightest attention? I want to believe it was just my natural needs that led me to be so stupid. After all, I haven't been with a man since well before we moved here, but I have a gnawing feeling there's more to it than that. All the passion left my body when Nick joined us on the dance floor and his hands found their way to my hips. I was just about to tell him so when a massive fight resulted in the entire club being shut down. Nick had to stay to help with clean-up, so I didn't get the chance to set things straight with him, and quite frankly I've been avoiding him all week. But today is the day I told him I would go to the brazilian jiu-jitsu class with him and then dinner this evening.

Sensing I'm not paying full attention to him, Trigger starts acting up. He cuts me off from his lunge and turns into me, almost barreling over me. I'm able to get out of his way, but it sets my head straight. I need to focus.

Chapter 11

Jace

Out of all the things going on in my life at this moment, having her show up at my Brazilian jiu-jitsu practice is something I would have never imagined. This week has been shit, from the brawl at the club to catching attitude from Marty. Not to mention that this fucking chick has been on my mind all week. It doesn't help that she came with Nick, or that she's looking as hot as ever. I'm thankful my cup hides my growth when I remember our shared breaths in the hallway.

Her black tank top is hanging low on her chest, revealing an elegant script tattoo. She's wearing red sweats that stretch nicely over her ass. What makes me smile is her camouflage hat that hides all her hair except for a dirty-blonde streak across her forehead. The hat emphasizes how large her ears are, and I realize with a start that this female is not someone I would normally go after. I watch as Alexis and Nick talk, and grow more agitated by the minute. He's a total putz for his continued efforts with her. I can tell she's not into him by her body language. She's closed off and disengaged as he jokes and hands her one of his uniforms. She slides the gi on over her clothes, and it hangs loosely from her body. As he helps her tie her belt, she angles her body away from him.

The professor begins the class, and I make sure to keep my distance. As Alexis steps onto the mats her eyes lock with mine and her entire body freezes. All my intentions of ingnoring her get tossed right out the fucking window. Winking at her is kinda my thing now, so I shoot her one for good measure. She rips her eyes from me as though I repulse her and plops down next to Nick. The gesture stings my pride. She focuses on the instructor and his lessons until I, more out of boredom than anything else, glance back at her and catch her staring. Adrenaline courses through my veins.

We're asked to partner up to practice the moves. Because I'm an assistant coach in class, various questions from students take over my immediate train of thought, though I watch her stretch from the corner of my eye. If the answers weren't burned into my brain, I may have stumbled on words.

For the partnered exercises a set group of students are asked to remain in one location while the other half rotates around. After the first round, I decide to stay where I am, knowing she will have to partner up with me eventually. Either she's ignoring that fact on purpose or she's extremely focused on learning jiu-jitsu.

Giving my partner only half my attention, I watch as she rolls with the person next to me. Using a lot of unnecessary energy, she fights hard against moves she doesn't understand how to properly get out of, and in the process, her belt comes untied. As the next match bell rings, signaling that it's time to switch, I calmly walk up to her, eyeing her every move. She sighs heavily, but her body moves a fraction of an inch toward mine. I bend to pick up her belt, never taking my eyes off hers. Her gaze quickly darts away, and I know the exchange has likely drawn Nick's attention.

Yet, she doesn't withdraw from me.

I go down on one knee before her, extending her belt around her waist, allowing my hands to drag open-palmed across her hips. She sucks in a breath, and I know then that her brusque attitude toward me is merely a show. I finish tying her belt and stand, looking down at her as her ice-blue eyes bore into mine. My stomach clenches, and I feel like someone has kicked me in the chest.

Turning away from her, I take a deep breath. I summon the memory of her fight with Simmons, remembering that Alexis is a wrestler. During her match she repeatedly avoided takedowns in favor of standing up to fight.

The buzzer sounds, letting everyone know

the matches have begun. They only last two minutes, which is plenty of time to unravel her a bit. Sometimes, I don't realize I'm being a dick, and sometimes I know exactly how my actions will be perceived.

I step back into a lazy stance, and she tries to mimic me. Her eyes are on mine—first mistake. She isn't watching my body. I fake a takedown, and she leans in just enough for me to grab her lapel. I step in to follow through, flip her over my hip, and deposit her hard onto the ground. She lands with a grunt.

I suck in a quick breath between my teeth. "Oh, wow. Your stance kinda sucks, kid."

She pops back up, sexual interest completely gone from her eyes. I can't help but flash my crooked smile at her irritation.

"Fuck you," she shoots back and immediately goes into game mode. Her gaze shifts to my chest, where it should have been in the first place. She can see my moves coming now...if she knows what to watch for.

I bait her with an outstretched arm. She grabs it greedily, thinking she has the advantage. Feigning resistance with a few tugs, she shifts her weight, not wanting to let go of her prize. I counterbalance my weight and pull her right into my guard. With a cocky grin I lock my feet behind her as she drops, stunned, between my open legs.

Her eyes narrow as she pushes her knees apart to maintain a good base. Her warmth against my body makes me grit my teeth to stay focused. She puts her hands on my hips, trying to break free. Her lapel drapes open again. I grab it and slowly pull her down on top of me until my breath is hot in her ear. Her hands relax on my hips, and her fingertips flex, almost like she wants to feel what's under my uniform. My dick twitches again within the confines of my cup. Her face is mere inches away, and I want to pull her lips into mine, if for nothing else but a repayment of her actions at the bar. Instead I slide my opposite hand under her arm, reaching back for her belt. With one hand locked on her lapel and the other on her belt, I buck my hips, rolling her onto her back. I keep from putting all my weight on her as I lean down and whisper, "Your base sucks too, kid."

Her breath is ragged, but she leans up slightly, eyes setting me on fire, and replies, "Fuck you." I'm taken aback by the promise in her voice, and a low growl slips past my lips.

Before I know it she bucks her hips and slides out from under me. She wraps her arms around me from behind and drives us both onto the mats. I land on my stomach, smiling like a halfwit, but quickly turn into her. She drops her weight on me, not quite getting the wet-blanket effect we teach in jiujitsu, but heavy enough to make me want to see what she's capable of. I allow her to mount me, knowing her arsenal of submissions is limited.

As soon as she sits up, her face goes blank, and a "what now" look flashes in her eyes. I place both hands on her hips and buck my own hips up into her ass. She falls forward, and I snake my arm up, wrapping it around her elbow joint and pulling, taking away her support and power. Tucking her arm to my chest, I arch my hips and roll us both over.

Coming up between her legs, I smile down on her. "I thought you had me there. What happened? Oh, wait—you wanted to fuck me, right?" I say as I lean into her with my hips, sliding my hands down her thighs.

Her face goes blank, and her body tightens under me. Damn, I may have gone too far. I relax my hold on her and begin to lean back. As I do, she squeezes her thighs, throwing me slightly off balance, allowing her just enough room to shift her hips, grab my arm, and pull me into an armbar.

Her legs tighten around my arm, and she thrusts her hips into the elbow joint of my arm, quickly resulting in a thoroughly painful situation. I momentarily try to fight it but end up having to tap out. She relieves some of the pressure from her hips but doesn't let go of my arm. Instead, she leans in and whispers with a tantalizingly seductive tone, "Fuck—you."

The buzzer sounds, and she holds onto my arm a moment longer, locking me in place with her storm-filled eyes. I know I must look like a lunatic, grinning up at her.

I wink and she releases me, then stands and mumbles under her breath. She walks straight past Nick and out of the gym, ignoring him as he tries to talk to her. I'm reeling as various emotions berate me. Though I know it's not my place, I find myself jumping up and following them out.

Chapter 12

Lexi

"Lexi, wait!" Nick jogs up behind me, putting his hand on my arm.

"Just leave it, Nick!"

"What happened in there? Did he hurt you?"

"No!" *God, no. He made me so damn wet and turned on, I almost kissed him right there in front of everyone!*

"Did he say something to you?"

Yes.

"No!" My internal conflict causes tears to prick the back of my eyes.

"Did I do something wrong?"

The concern in his voice stops me in my tracks. Softening my voice, I turn to face him, blinking the moisture away rapidly. "No, Nick, you didn't do anything, I just...I..."

"Hey, it's okay. I get how ridiculous that guy can be. Add that on top of it being your first day in class; I get it." Nick steps up to me, wrapping me in a hug, and stupidly I allow it. Desire and anger swirl within me. I want to be comforted, but I know leading him on is wrong—which is why I have to make things clear at dinner.

I pull away and force a grin. "See you to-night?"

"Yeah, see you tonight." He gives me one of his flawless smiles while he squeezes my elbow slightly, then heads for his car.

I run a hand down my face and growl into the evening air.

"I am totally impressed right now."

I whip around.

"Not only do you have a mean armbar, but you are totally a player." The source of all my conflict stares at me, completely shirtless with both hands hanging onto a tree limb above him. He leans forward, and his whole midsection flexes.

I actually have to close my eyes moment-arily before responding. "One, I'm not a player." I open them and take in his tattoo-covered form. He is beautiful. Dark hair lies across his forehead. A mischievous look glints in his eyes. "Two, it's absolutely none of your business." He saunters for-ward, and heat blooms in my stomach.

"I don't know. I mean, you were there earl-ier, right? You felt that between us?" He looks at me with his stupid crooked smile, and I want to punch him.

"The only thing between us back there was your ego and your fucked-up mind games." I try to put conviction into my words, but as he continues to stalk forward my voice loses its edge.

Now only a foot away, he stares down at me, and I try not to let the closeness affect my breathing. "No, you see, I wanted to see what you were capable of, and I was just telling the truth. I figured you were simply doing the same. Your jiujitsu sucks. You should let me give you some lessons."

My pride stings, and I grit my teeth. "If it sucks so bad, how did I get you in an armbar? Oh wait, let me guess, you let me."

Jace steps closer, and my body reacts on its on, like a magnet is pulling me toward him. It's like I'm suspended in space, fighting not to slam into his alluring force field. "Uh, surprisingly no. You totally caught me off-guard—I'll give you that —but it won't happen again. I can guarantee it. At least not until you surpass your master."

You're damn right I caught you off-guard. At his admission, I try... I really try to keep the smile from gracing my lips, but here I stand, smiling at this infuriating madman.

"Look, you're going to school here. You're a fighter. You have lots of potential, and you're nice to look at. All I see is a win-win-win in you joining the club."

I have to walk away from him before I do something stupid, and of course he follows me. *Can you not tell I want to fuck you? Now please leave me alone before I do something I'll regret later.*

"Next practice is Monday," he says as I climb

into my truck. "I have a gi you can have. That one sucks." He points to the uniform still wrapped around me like a blanket. "Kinda like your ground game, kid."

He starts to lean into the window, and I open the door quickly, hitting him in the knees. "Don't call me kid," I toss out the window as I start the truck and drive away, smiling as I watch him jump around in my rearview mirror.

∞∞∞

"Love, I have to stop you. You've been going on about this dude for almost an hour."

Ann's statement has me gawking, and I shoot her a defensive glare. "No I haven't."

She sighs and taps her phone, showing me the screen.

"Oh my God! I have. I have to go get ready for dinner with Nick."

"What? Um, no. You promised me that you would go to that party with me tonight."

"That's not until next week."

"Alexis Mae Trucco! I asked you last Thursday. I told you it was a week out. You said okay. It's been a week. I don't want to go to this thing by myself! I told you that guy from Algebra invited me, and I don't want to give the goods away if I get too wasted! I need you as my winglady."

"What am I going to do about Nick? I need

to let him know I don't have feelings for him like that."

"Feelings like you have for Jace Boston?"

I throw my water bottle at her. "Annabelle!"

"Fine! Fine. Why don't you just invite him to go with us?"

I pause, playing out the scenario in my head. "I suppose I could. It would be less intimate than just the two of us going to dinner. Okay, I'll call him. But I swear, if you ditch me for this dude tonight, I am going to shave your head in your sleep."

Ann fake gasps. "I cannot believe you think I would allow my lady loins to control my actions like that!"

I purse my lips at her.

"Okay, fine! I will wear my chastity belt. You happy?"

"Ecstatic."

"Oh, that reminds me! What did you do with that pack of condoms we bought the other day?" I leap from the couch and pounce on her as she squeals. "I kid, I KID! Lexi, I am going to pee on you!"

∞∞∞

Sitting outside the massive oceanside condo, I turn to Ann. "How long do you think we've been sitting here?"

"Twenty minutes at least. We cannot go in

yet! Maybe we just drive around for a little bit?"

So far we've only seen people bringing in massive amounts of liquor but no actual party-goers. "If we drive around, we may get lost, which was why we left so early in the first place."

"It's also why we're here half an hour before the party is supposed to start." Ann sighs. "If we go in now, we'll look like total pips."

"If we sit here and stare at this house any longer, we're going to look like creepy pips."

Ann sighs again with more dramatic flair. "Okay, fine. One more touch-up and we can go in."

She's wearing a silky baby-blue top that flows from her shoulders and elegantly lies across her chest. With her white hip-huggers and soft curls, she's sure to be one of the prettiest girls here. I, on the other hand, managed to escape her insistence that I should dress up a little more, with only a little mascara and eyeliner as a compromise. I'm wearing my black wifebeater, a push-up bra, blue jean shorts, and a pair of cowboy boots.

"Maybe we just wait another ten minutes," I offer her after she finishes applying another layer of lip gloss.

"Nope, you're right. If we wait any longer, someone is going to call the cops on us, and the fun will be over before we've even done anything worthy of having the cops called on us for." Ann flips the visor closed. "Now, get your tooshie out of this truck."

The house is magnificent. The bottom story

is painted a deep red. Four pillars stand near a double staircase that leads to an upper level where we watched all the alcohol disappear while we were sitting in the truck.

Slowly climbing the steps, I take in the view. Behind the house the ocean crashes gently into the beautiful sand-covered beach. A group of people are putting together a woodpile for a bonfire. Breaking waves reflect the nearly full moon. Laid out before us is the bar of all bars, housing every drink imaginable. Ann and I exchange a look and squeal.

After we each get our drink of choice we start exploring the house. People have begun filing in. Soon Ann's manly friend shows up and introduces himself to me. "Hi, I'm Val." He's clean-cut and is wearing a blazer over a V-neck T-shirt. Not bad on the eyes,but his wrists would likely snap if he were to punch someone.

I extend my hand. "Lexi." His grip is weak, and his eyes dart away from mine.

Ann places her hand on his arm. "Thank you so much for inviting us to this party. This place is absolutely wondrous."

"It's okay I suppose. I own about five of them up and down the coast. This one is a closet compared to them, truth be told."

My stomach churns at his hoity attitude. So when my phone starts singing "Hell on wheels" by Miranda Lambert I'm both irritated by the look on his face and relieved for an excuse to get away from him.

"I have to take this. Um, don't go far without me, okay? I could easily get lost in this little
closet." I sneer as the guy turns to walk away, and
Ann shrugs a shoulder. Shaking my head, I walk
out onto the balcony to answer my phone. "Hey,
Mom, how are you? Where are you now?"

"Hey, John and I just left Florida. It was so
clammy. Have you seen the wildlife there? And
the girls, walking around half naked all the time.
I mean, if I looked like that I would be too, but
still!"

She isn't actually asking questions for me to
answer, so I choose to say, "Sounds like you're enjoying yourself. Where are you headed next?"

"Our plan is to hit Vegas. We were going to
save it until last, but Florida wasn't much fun, so
John is taking me there next." Mom has been with
John for a little over three years now. He's okay.
He treats Mom like a queen, and I love that about
him. He got hurt last year on the job and got a
huge settlement, so now he and Mom are "keeping
it loose" as he would say. Thinking about it now
makes me shudder.

Mom deserves it though. We moved around
a lot when I was a kid. She's never liked staying in
one spot. So traveling suits her. I haven't heard her
this happy in a long time.

"How are you, sweetheart? How did your
fight go? I knew you would win. I really wish I had
been there. How is Grandpa's farm doing, and my

Kitty girl?"

I sigh, wondering where to start. She dislikes me fighting, and although she brought it up, I know anything I say about it will be pushed straight out the other side of the phone into the stagnant Florida air. So instead of correcting her about my loss, I change the subject. "Kitty is wonderful. She misses you. I'm good, started classes a few weeks ago." Turning around, I lean against the balcony. My voice trails off as I see Jace Boston talking to Ann. She points my way.

Traitor.

"Uh...hey, Mom. I am so sorry, but I'm going to have to call you back. How does tomorrow sound?"

"Oh, shoot, I always forget that we're in a different time zone. I forgot how late it is there. Okay, my sweet girl. Talk to you tomorrow. Love you."

"Love you too, Momma." Pressing the end button, I turn back to look out over the ocean. I hear Jace's footfalls as he walks up behind me, and my heart rate accelerates.

"Am I interrupting something?"

"You are." What is it about this man that unravels me at the seams?

"Oh? Is that so?" He joins me as I look out at the bonfire starting up below. "I just want you to know, I have bruises on my shins from your little stunt with the door."

"Yeah. Well, you know what they say about

assholes."

Humor dances in his eyes. "No. What do they say?"

"Uh..." I didn't expect him to follow up. "Well, you know...that you need to hit 'em with your car doors."

His laugh is ominous and yet beautiful. It infects me, and I find myself laughing too. His eyebrows pull together like the action is something foreign to him, uncomfortable even. Yet, as the laugh escapes into the wind, his body relaxes. I stare at him with amusement.

He coughs, looking down for a moment. Then his eyes lift to mine.

Chapter 13

Jace

I have tried all day to get her off my mind, and I intended to come to this party and get lost in some bird's feathers tonight. Yet here she is *again*, and I stupidly left the two girls who were talking to me as soon as I saw her friend, Ann. I keep thinking about how it felt to have her lips on mine, how her body responded to my every touch. I have to keep myself from asking her stupid questions like what her favorite movie is. Or her middle name. Such mundane questions, such personal questions. I fail to wrap my mind around why I'm doing this to myself. I want to leave. I want to get as far away from her as I can, but her eyes keep drawing me in. I know I should be a dick and say something true to character like "Nice tits," but instead I hand her the drink in my hand and say, "Disaronno and Dr. Pepper, right?"

She smiles and takes it, whispering a small "Thank you." She takes a sip, then says, "You have a lovely laugh." Her words pull me back to reality, and I set my jaw, barely refraining from saying something stupid. Then an irritated voice cuts into my personal dilemma.

"Lexi."

Nick walks out onto the balcony, and suddenly the space feels small. My previous joke about her being a player bites me in the ass. *Who's laughing now, huh, smart-ass?*

"Hey, Nick. I looked for you when we first got here but couldn't find you," she says as she walks over to him.

He steps closer, pulling her into a hug. "Ann and Val are heading down to the bonfire. Want to join them?"

She glances back at me, appearing torn.

Nick sucks in a breath, and I laugh at his weakness. "You are such a douchebag, Norsby," I say, pushing off the balcony. I walk straight up to him. Watching the fear light up in his eyes makes bile rise in my throat. I cut my eyes to Alexis. "You sure do know how to lead people on." I clench my teeth as I walk away, a cold sensation kissing my neck as I look for the bottle of Jack on the open bar.

Walking seemed like a good idea. Being alone was preferable until this bird took it upon herself to "keep me company." My mood is shit, and the copious amount of liquor I'm consuming has done little to help that fact. When she begins asking personal questions, which I loathe, I quickly tell her to kick rocks. My head feels light, so I sit down, pushing my toes deep into the sand. Because I grew up on the coast, I often wonder what it would be like to live anywhere else. Somewhere that actually has seasons, no earthquakes. Maybe even a place where no one knows my name.

A hand touches my shoulder, and a voice says, "Boo." I jerk forward, fists raised. The newcomer jumps back a few paces. I'm more surprised by the fact that someone was able to sneak up on me than the simple tap on the shoulder.

"Seriously, you swing first, ask questions later?" Alexis crosses her arms, looking both amused and upset.

Suddenly I wish my buzz were not wearing off.

"Yeah, something like that," I mumble and turn back to the darkness.

She comes and sits down next to me.

I press my chin to my shoulder, looking over at her with hazy eyes. Despite my irritation at her interest in Norsby, her presence lifts my mood, and I begin drinking it in. "Where is your Nose?" I ask, amusing myself with my own cleverness.

Her hand lifts and touches her nose, confused. Then she smiles knowingly at me. "Funny— but a player doesn't pick her nose and tell."

"Ah, so you picked him, huh?"

Lexi sighs. "I didn't know there was more than one nose to pick."

I shrug, very aware that my liquor is talking for me. "Maybe not a nose, but there could be an ass."

Both of us burst out laughing. She snorts, and we laugh harder. I haven't laughed this much since I was a kid. She falls back onto the sand, tensing up, and says, "Instant regret."

"Yeah, that bad, huh?"

"No, the sand. I hate sand." She sits up, trying to eradicate the sand from her back and shoulders. "I don't even know why I agreed to come down here."

"Here." I scoot around and help her brush it away. My hand touches her warm skin, and sobriety hits me like a truck. A small noise escapes her lips as she leans into my open palm. When I reach out to pull her into me, she jerks forward.

"Where did they go?" Her head swivels left and right.

"Where did who go?" I ask, brushing my hand off on my shorts.

"Ann and that dude she was with." She stands. "They were supposed to wait for me by the bonfire."

My eyes quickly scan the handful of people gathered near the flames. Ann is not there. Lexi pulls out her phone and starts for the house. I jump up and start after her, leaving my sandals behind.

"Maybe she had to use the bathroom?" Even

as I say it, I have an uneasy sensation. I pull my phone from my pocket, clicking out a quick message to Ty. When Ann doesn't answer Lexi's call we begin searching the bathrooms on the ground level. Nothing. We head to the lower level of the house, where people normally go to hook up. I open the first door as Lexi continues down the hall. After seeing no sign of Ann, I pull the door closed on a baffled couple scrambling to cover up.

Turning my attention back to the hallway, I realize Lexi has disappeared. My heart begins to slow as I take in everything around me. My eyes snap to a door slightly ajar. I bolt forward when I hear a loud yell.

"Jace?" I hear Tyler's voice behind me as I throw open the door. Ann is lying across the bed, still fully clothed but unmoving. I watch as her chest dips and rises slowly. At first I don't see Lexi. Then, as I push farther into the room, I see legs sprawled and thrashing in the bathroom. I rush forward with a red veil over my eyes that gets ripped away when I enter. Lexi is on top of Val—whose pants are down around his ankles—raining punches down on his face while he bleeds freely all over his fancy clothing.

Ty stands in the doorway to the room looking back and forth between the girl and me. "Get Ann out to the car." Nodding at my order, he strides forward, lifting her with ease. Her head lolls to the side; she's mumbling incoherently. He shushes her and carries her out the door.

Stepping into the bathroom, I get close enough so I can intervene if necessary. Val's nose looks broken. I reach to pull Lexi off him, knowing this is the kind of dude who will try to press charges even though he completely deserves this. As I wrap my arms around her, she begins kicking and screaming for me to let her go.

"I'll kill you! Do you hear me? I swear to God, I will kill you, you disgusting waste of life!" She spits on tile, missing her pussified target.

"Lexi!" I flip her around to face me. "Lexi, stop!" I shake her slightly, and she throws her arms up, shoving me back.

Her eyes are dilated, and she inhales deeply like the wind has gotten knocked back into her. "Where is Ann?" I watch as the white hot fury gives way to fear in her eyes. Blood drips from her busted knuckles.

Val whimpers behind her and gets to his feet, lunging at her. I take one giant step forward and throw all my weight into my punch. The connection results in Val instantly crumpling to the ground.

"What the hell did you do that for?" Lexi rounds on me, hurt flashing in her eyes. I know she's emotional and possibly blaming herself, but her words slap me in the face. She pushes past me, and I grit my teeth. I flip Val onto his side and dig inside his pockets, pulling a small plastic baggy out. I kick him one more time as I identify two roofies.

Outside, Lexi seems to have calmed some-
what—either that or she's great at slipping on a
mask. I approach with caution.

"Is she going to be okay?" she asks Ty, who
shoots me a look.

"She was roofied." I toss the baggie to Ty.
"She needs to rest, but she should be fine."

Tyler takes off his jacket and covers Ann
with it. "Why don't you let us take you two home?
I can help get her inside," Tyler offers.

She hesitates, so I add, "I'll have Cooper
bring your truck over in the morning."

Lexi nods and climbs into the back seat with
Ann, lifting her head onto her lap. I almost snap
seeing the girl so helpless.

"Jace, don't do it." Tyler locks eyes with me
over the top of the car. He leans forward. "Cooper
hasn't bought this house yet. We don't have security here, so don't. It isn't worth it. Just get in the
car and let's take them home."

I clench my fists, getting into the car. I look
into the rearview mirror as Ty puts the car in
drive. Lexi looks up. There's blood dripping from
her eye.

*That motherfucker hit her. He actually fucking
hit her!* I bite hard on my cheek, tasting the salty,
metallic tang of blood. I open my door.

Ty grabs me. "Don't fucking do it!"

I jerk my arm away and jump from the car as
Ty tries to take off, thinking that will stop me.

Halfway up the steps, a small force collides

into my chest.

"Stop!" Lexi's hands are on me, shoving me back.

I look at her with wide eyes.

"Stop! He isn't worth it, and I shouldn't be here trying to tell you this. I should be back there with her!" Tears fill her eyes, and the pain in them hits me like a Taser. For the first time in my life I find myself walking away from a fight, and I can't describe the emotions swirling around inside me.

Chapter 14

Lexi

P ure, unfiltered hate courses through my veins. Ann holds her breath for a few heart-beats, and the hate morphs into fear. Fear so deep and strong it's like someone slid an ice-cold knife into my heart. My skin breaks out in gooseflesh. I try to avoid Jace's eyes. The emotion in them makes me feel sick. I can't tell if he's angry with me for stopping him from finishing off Val or if he's worried. I hate that he might be worried about me. I don't deserve it. It's my fault this happened. He should be worried about Ann, not me. Nothing horrifying happened to me. How am I going to explain this to her? How will I be able to make her understand how sorry I am? A creeping sensation that the car is shrinking envelops my mind. All at once the space is too small, and I can't breathe.

We reach the farm, and I exhale heavily into the crisp night air. Ty pulls Ann easily from the

car and carries her inside and upstairs. I follow
close behind. Standing in her doorway, I begin to
break. Ty lays her on the bed and slips past me,
back downstairs. I walk over to her, watching her
breathe. I don't know how long I stay that way, but
when she finally opens her eyes and looks at me,
I crumple to my knees. Burying my head into her
blankets, I let the sobs rattle my body. She shushes
me, patting my head with a shaky hand.

"I am so sorry, Annabelle. I should've never
left you. I-I..." I can't talk through my shame, and
Ann selflessly lets me get it all out, rubbing my
back as I cry.

When the sobs slow, she says, "This was not
your fault, love." My gaze falls on her eyes; they
drift open and closed. The sight steels me, draining the desire to cry from my body. She is drugged,
exhausted, and yet she is comforting me.

I wipe my nose and ask, "Is there anything I
can get for you?"

Ann shakes her head. "Right now all I want to
do is sleep."

I nod and stand to leave. Before I even make
it out the door her light snores drift to meet my
ears. Reaching the kitchen, I begin to hyperven-
tilate, then push out the back door. The cool air
runs its fingers through my hair as I bolt into the
barn. My fists find the homemade punching bag,
and a flurry of punches and kicks erupts from my
body like lava from a volcano. I'm flailing haphaz-
ardly, making the bag whistle with each landed

strike, stopping only when I can't raise my arms and my legs are like lead. Blood drips from my raw knuckles. Small divots form in the sand with each fallen drop. Acid rises in the back of my throat as images from the night's events flash across my mind. *I should have killed him.*

"You should let me look at your eye." I might have jumped if my body wasn't so drained. The worried note in Jace's voice makes me lash out.

"What are you still doing here? You did your honorable thing. You can leave now."

He stays there, silent and unmoving. Immediately I regret my words. Yet I cannot take them back, so the silence stretches on.

"A farm, huh? I would love to see this in the daylight." The sincerity in his voice shreds my remaining remorse, leaving me empty and exhausted.

"It's my Grandpa's, or it was... He passed away and left it to me."

Jace nods and steps out from the shadows into a sliver of moonlight filtering through the open door.

I fight the urge to want to be comforted by him.

"I want to protect you." His admission throws me for a loop.

"From what? If you haven't noticed, I can protect myself just fine. It's the people I care about that I can't protect."

His clenched jaw is evident even in the dim

light. "You have no idea how much I understand what you just said. Yet, it doesn't diminish my desire to protect you, even knowing deep down I truly can't. No one can fully protect anyone in this world."

Somehow his words resonate within me. "Maybe it's not the act of actually protecting those you care about, but the effort to at least try."

His mood becomes broody when his cell phone dings in his pocket. His eyes are dark and ominous as they hungrily stare at me.

"Are you going to get that? It could be your brother."

Jace moves toward me like a predator stalking its prey. "Do you want me to answer it?"

Confusion clouds my mind. "I don't know. Is it important?" As he steps closer, I stand my ground.

"Do you know what it would mean if I ignored this text...for you...because of you?"

The scent of his breath fills my lungs. I inhale deeply, trying to understand his meaning. "Jace, I don't know what you're talking about."

Slowly he leans down, pressing his forehead against my own. I close my eyes, relishing the connection of our skin. "You are such a stubborn female, a badass but stubborn female."

Pulling away, he lifts his hand. Something white is clenched in his fist. He dabs the gauze against my split eyebrow; it smells of antiseptic, and a sharp sting shoots to the back of my eye.

"Ouch! Shit, that hurt." I jerk away, and he smiles.

"It's not the action of actually protecting those you care about, it's the effort of trying. Isn't that right?"

I smile up at him through one eye. As he turns to leave, he stops at the door and, without looking back, says, "Just remember, I'm the ass-hole, okay?" Then, out into the moonlit night he goes, leaving me with a hurricane of emotions.

Back in the house I cook some bland eggs and get a glass of gatorade, trying to coax Ann to get something into her system. Mainly to shut me up, she takes a bite of the eggs and a sip of gatorade be-fore drifting back to sleep. I watch her for a while, thinking how much worse tonight could have gone. Then I curl up next to her in case she needs me in the next few hours, before the sun comes up.

∞∞∞

For the next few days Ann is still kinda out of it, and we both call into school sick. Nick offers to bring us all the classwork we're missing, while apologizing profusely that he wasn't there when I needed him. I reassure him without rubbing the fact that Jace was there in his face, though some-thing in his voice hints that he already knows.

It appears the events from that night were harder on me than Ann—that or she's turning everything into a joke to hide how she really feels about it.

"I mean, seriously, if Val wanted in my pants that bad he could've just asked." Ann, who is leaning on the gate, gives a weak laugh.

I roll my eyes at her as I brush Trigger.

"We all know how dry my lady bits had become, so yeah, I was a little thirsty," she adds.

I shake my head. "I'm having a hard time finding the humor in this. I mean, I still want to kill that dirtbag."

"Oh no, he's gotten what he deserves. I heard from the grapevine that he got another ass whooping the next day. He didn't even have time to recover from the one you dealt him."

"Yeah, who did you hear that from?" I pause my brushing and look over at her.

"Oh, you know…Tyler Boston." Ann bobs her head and purses her lips together like its a casual thing.

I can't help but grin as I realize who she's been texting all week, all the while with a fat smile on her face. "Well, hopefully he isn't anything like his brother." I turn back to brushing Trigger.

"Still no word from Jace?"

"Nope, and sadly, I don't expect to hear from him."

"But you want to."

I sigh, giving up on the task at hand. "Of course I want to." Realization hits me. "Wait, so was that Tyler the other day when you said 'the Mormons' were at the front door and you would handle them? Then stayed outside talking to them for half an hour?"

Ann didn't even try to lie. "Well...I knew if I said that, you wouldn't come bother us. Besides, you were still upset about Jace, and I wanted to protect you."

I smile at her words.

"What?" she asks.

I shake my head. "Nothing, just something Jace said the last time I saw him."

"Since we're on the topic of Boston brothers...Ty has asked me out on a date this weekend..." Ann smiles at me innocently.

I laugh and whip the end of my lunge rope at her. Trigger's ears perk up, and he takes off at a perfect trot around the pen.

"Oh, now you want to do what I ask." Ann and I both laugh as we head inside for lunch.

∞∞∞

Saturday evening comes, and I find myself trying desperately to avoid getting asked for any sort of fashion advice while nursing my own wounds of rejection.

Ann stands in front of her full-length mirror, covered only by a towel, brushing different magic powders onto her face. "Why don't you call Nick, maybe go see a movie or something?" She studies her appearance with one eye closed. "Maybe you were wrong about him. I mean, he has been around a lot lately."

"He just feels bad that he left us at the party," I say while pondering her words. "I don't know, I just didn't have that—"

"Vagina-clenching feeling with him like you did with Jace?"

I pause just before taking a sip of my pop. "Yeah...took the words right outta my mouth."

Ann shrugs. "How do you know you don't have that feeling with Nick? You haven't even really given him a chance. I mean, did you jump him in a bathroom hallway and shove your tongue down his throat? Did you dry hump him on some fighting mats? Did you—"

"Gah, you make me sound horrible! That's not how any of that happened, you dramatic cob-goblin."

Ann stops her primping and looks at me. "You need to listen to me. Give him another chance. I hate seeing you all crusty like this."

I roll my eyes. "Yes, and your advice is what exactly?"

"Hump him."

I laugh. "Is that how your night is going to go? Humping Ty?"

The doorbell chimes. Ann pops up to her feet. "Shit, what time is it?"

I look at my phone. "It's eight o'clock."

"Seriously? He's on time. Who shows up to a date on time? Urgh, can you stall him for me, doll face?" She holds up two dresses in front of the mirror, and I bolt down the stairs before she has a chance to say, "Red or blue?"

Swinging the heavy oak door open, I'm greeted with a dazzling smile. Instantly I note how similar Ty and Jace look. Their eyes are the same shade of hazel, but Jace has a smattering of golden flakes in his. Their eyebrows arch in the same way, and they both have that cocky, crooked grin.

"Hey, Alexis."

"Hey, Ty. Ann will be down in, uh, I don't know how long she'll be. Wanna come in and have some coffee?"

Tyler's brows furrow together as he enters the house. "Sure, but I'm confused. She said to pick her up at eight."

We walk into the kitchen, and I pour two cups. After adding fixings to my own, I offer them to him, and he shakes his head, taking his black.

"Yeah, when she says eight, she means eight fifteen. She's still naked up there."

Ty smiles, unfazed by my teasing. He looks at me for a long moment, and an awkward silence stretches before us.

"What?" I laugh nervously.

"Jace, he doesn't do well with—"

I raise my hand. "Stop. Don't be his messenger. If he wants to say something to me, he needs to man up and do it himself."

Ty watches me for a moment, then nods. His eyes shift to look past me. He releases a low whistle. I turn to see Ann, thankful she didn't ask my opinion, 'cause the blue dress looks stunning on her.

"Have her back by midnight!" I holler as Ann waves and they head out the door.

I flip open my phone and scroll down to Nick's number. I note that no vagina clenching happens, so I flip it closed with a sigh and head upstairs.

I leap onto my bed with a few bounces and reach for the book on my nightstand. After a few moments of letting my mind wander, I huff and switch my book out for my journal, deciding to work on a book idea that's been drifting around in my head. Not five minutes pass before my phone chirps. I look down to see my sister's name on the screen.

"Hey, Sis, what's up?" I have one older sister and two older brothers. They're Marie and Paul's natural children and my adoptive siblings, but I'm their baby sis, all the same.

"Hey, Sister. Uh…is Ann there? Are you guys home?" Something in her voice sends a jolt of panic through my body.

"Ann is out for the night, but yes, I'm home. Why? What's wrong? Kate, what happened?"

Silence wraps its cold fingers around my heart and squeezes. "Oh, Sister…" Pain makes her voice tremble, and I can hear her fighting back her emotions. My mind starts flicking through one heartbreaking scenario to another like a horror film montage. I want to hang up. If I hang up now, I won't have to know. If I don't hear it, it won't be real.

I feel like my voice is only a whisper, but the words fly out of me in loud squeaks. "Kate! Is it Mom? Please, please don't say it's Mom—" My own anticipation cuts me off as my eyes fill with premature tears.

Our mother, my savior, has a number of health problems. She had her first heart attack when I was five, then two more after she and Dad divorced. I couldn't bear it—I can't lose her. First Grandpa, and now this? No, not my mommy. She raised me, and I put her through hell in my early teens. I was so broken after my dad gave up his rights to me and started a new family, that I lashed out at her. I'm still trying to make up for it all. I'm not done trying to make up for it all...

"Sister...something awful has happened."

Chapter 15

Jace

I tried. I really did. I got lost in bird feathers, in fighting, in training. I even took a drive up to our mountain cabin. Nothing has eradicated her from my thoughts. My mind keeps replaying that night, that specific moment I got a message from Marty. I was supposed to drop everything and take care of business, like I have so many times before, but I stalled. I didn't want to go.

She will know only pain if I allow myself to have feelings for her. She would hate me if she knew what really went on in my life. Things are too fucked up, and I hate it. Why would I subject someone else to it when I'm searching for a way out? She deserves things I can never give her.

Ty took Ann out to dinner. Then he was supposed to bring her to the club. He isn't ashamed of our life; he's actually excited to share it with Ann. So when he told me he saw Lexi, I thought that I would put her quality of life first. Yeah, right. I curse my selfishness as I sit on my motorcycle and stare at her darkened house. Maybe she isn't home. Maybe she's gone out for a night with Norsby.

I kick my stand out and swing my leg over. As my foot reaches the front step, the door falls open. A beautiful disaster stares down at me with hooded eyes. My breath catches in my throat, and my resolve breaks then and there.

"Alexis—" She's been crying; her eyes are red and swollen. Her proud shoulders slump forward. I scale the last few steps and stand before her. Her raw grief split me in two, and I grapple with my words. "What, I—"

Fuck.

I should leave, now...

Her breathing is labored, and the fumes that waft toward me alert my senses to pay attention, snapping me from my stupor. "Alexis, what's wrong? What happened?"

"Why are you here?" The venom in her words bites into my stomach.

I say nothing.

"Do you love your father?" she asks. The hoarseness in her voice knocks the air out of me, while her words confuse me.

"I don't know my father." She's pulled the truth from me without even trying.

"That would make things easier." She turns and leaves me standing in the open doorway. I step into the chilly house, closing the door behind me. I find her in the kitchen with a half-empty bottle of whisky sitting in front of her.

Her eyes roam over me, watching for my reaction. I keep my face blank as I take a seat across from her. I need to know what's going on to understand how to best respond to her anguish.

"It must be nice, being able to shut people out so easily." Blue iris voids stare at me, daring me to deny it.

"It's a gift and a curse," I admit, and I can see it stings her. I grit my teeth. "Will you please tell me what's wrong?"

She stands, her chair screeching away from her with force. "I don't need your protection. I don't need your attempts at protection. There is nothing you could have done or can do now to help me!" She paces on unsteady legs, and I stand, ready to make her understand. I want to try to make her understand. Sighing, I realize there's truly nothing I can do or say. She walks away from me, growls, and turns back. One foot snags behind the other. Her reaction is slow, but her body slips down quickly. I reach out, wrapping my arms around her as if I've done it a thousand times.

Her body doesn't respond to my touch, and the stiffness that greets me pricks little holes in my lungs. Then all at once she crumples into me, and sobs wrack her body. I pull her into me, squeezing her like I'm trying to keep her from breaking into a million pieces.

Her breathless voice breaks through her pained cries in small waves. "He was my hero... He was my everything... I...I did everything just to... make him proud of me... To prove I was worth having as a daughter..." Her words slowly put together a grief-stricken picture. "But it wasn't enough...and now...he is—" She jerks from my arms, but not far enough, as puke splatters across my pants and boots. I shift her so she's facing the sink as massive amounts of liquid expel from her small frame. After her stomach is empty, she continues to dry heave until her body stills.

"Oh, God! I am so sorry, Jace." Her words echo slightly from within the sink, and I smile.

"Hey, at least I didn't have to hold your hair back." I reach to pull her into me again, but the mess between us makes me pause. "We need to get you cleaned up, and I need to, uh, clean up a bit myself. You up for a shower?—I mean by yourself, not together or anything... I just need to use your washer."

"Okay." She doesn't even have the fight in her to tell me to fuck off, and I'm thankful. When she lifts her head to look at me, my heart drops into the pit of my stomach. Her eyes glisten, and her hair sticks to her forehead. Pain is etched so deep in her eyes, I fear it will stay there forever. This strong, steadfast woman is broken, and I feel exposed by the way my own emotions are responding. I become locked in her gaze as her eyes bore into mine, like she can see everything that makes me...me. Uncomfortable, I look away. No one should have to endure being inside my head or meeting my soul.

I step away from her and extend my hand, gesturing for her to lead the way. Upstairs, she points to a small room. "You can wash your pants in there." As she continues down the hall on wobbly legs, she calls back, "Everything you need is above the washer in the cupboard. Pull the knob hard, and just before you feel like it's going to break, it will turn on."

I quickly toss in my shirt and pants and flick in a bit of detergent. Then I grab the knob after switching the setting to quick wash and small. I pull, testing its limits, but nothing happens. Putting some force into it, I hear the machine come to life right as the damn thing breaks clean off.

Fuck.

Well, at least this load will be washed. I'll buy her a new fucking machine.

I go back into the hallway and hear a low rumbling. Following the noise, I end up in the open doorway of the bathroom. "Hey, uh, I just started the washer. Your hot water may not last long," I warn. Now that the knob is missing, I have no idea how to turn it off.

"At this point I think a cold one would do more good." She laughs, and I desperately wish I could see the smile on her face.

A few minutes pass, and the water shuts off. I turn away toward the hallway for a moment, but my caveman side calls me a bitch, and I glance back. A pale hand snakes out from the curtains, grabbing a towel from the hook conveniently placed within arm's length.

She steps out with a towel around her. Her hair clings to her head, water trickling down her face. She ducks her head and starts to walk out of the bathroom, but I step into her path. I'm only wearing my boxers and socks while she stands there dripping. "Do you want me to wait down-stairs?" My voice comes out low and full of primal need. She lifts a hand, placing it on my bare chest, and I wonder if she notices the effect it has on me. Her eyes widen. The thin fabric of my boxers doesn't hide my growing erection, and the pressure from her hand increases, pushing me backward. When there's enough space, she slips away from me and down the hall. I follow, only to get a door slammed in my face.

I knock, and a grin spreads across my face. "Come on, I won't look...twice," I lie. A few minutes pass, and I refrain from swinging the door open after I hear a few loud bangs. Then the door creaks open marginally.

Inside, Lexi is under her giant fluffy covers. My smile fades. She looks so small and fragile. I walk forward slowly, giving her time to tell me to fuck off. Then I simply stand there, like a god-damn idiot. She sighs and, without turning to face me, pulls the covers back, revealing thick hips and a perfect body clothed in a tank top and under-wear. I sit down next to her, my mind racing. Her body trembles next to mine, and I push my legs under the blanket against hers. Wrapping my arms around her, I pull her into me.

"Do you want to talk about what happened?" I ask, knowing how things like this can chip away at a person's sanity.

She breathes heavily. "They couldn't tell me much, but my father is dead, and the cops suspect foul play. Other than that, they told me I had to wait until the investigation was over, and I really don't want to talk about it."

"You don't have to talk to me about it, but will you talk to Ann tomorrow?"

She nods and grabs my hand from around her waist, pulling it to rest under her chin. Her breathing slowly becomes even as she drifts off to sleep.

Soon, she grows restless and twitches in my arms. As she turns into me, she lays her head on my chest and wraps her arms around me. I've never been in this position with any other female willingly. I breathe deeply, committing her scent to memory, and press my lips to her forehead. It isn't even midnight before I hear my phone going off. I growl into the darkness and pull away from Lexi's warmth to grab it. My mind slowly begins shutting off my emotions as I prepare for the consequences of my actions.

I grip my phone tighter, frustrated that this is happening now. As the power fades from the phone, I place it back on the nightstand and turn back into the sleeping form next to me, not allowing my mind to think of what tomorrow may bring.

Chapter 16

Lexi

The beach lies before us. Jace sits inches away from me, flexing his toes in the sand. Ann is safe with Ty, and the glow from the fire lights up her face as she laughs. Jace looks out over the ocean while I steal glances at him. In the moonlight he looks sinister, sexy, like a forbidden fruit. His dark hair drapes lazily across his forehead. A tattoo snakes out from the neck of his white tee. His knees are bent, hands clasped together on top of them. His eyes are so dark they could pass as black except that the yellowish specks in them give the illusion they're glowing faintly.

He shifts position, and we lock eyes. The attraction is so thick in the air you can almost see it spark as it bounces between us. His eyes rake over me, seeing everything I am. All the dysfunction, all the mental instability. Yet his eyes dilate with need. My core quivers when his gaze drops to my lips. Gliding my tongue across them, I wade into my own building desires. He leans in, and a crooked smile graces his moistened lips. His warm, sweet-scented breath tickles my face. I close my eyes, the passion inside me impatient for the distance between us to vanish.

Our lips touch, and heat rips throughout my body and shoots to the slippery cleft between my legs. My thighs become antsy as they moisten at the center. Parting my lips, I welcome his tongue, which tastes like grape mixed with a sweetness all his own. His hand glides up to hold my cheek as the kiss intensifies, his tongue expertly massaging mine. I squeeze my knees together to try and quiet the pleading from between them.

Smoothing his hand out to cup my neck, he drops his kisses to my jawline. Tilting my head to the side, I give him room to do what he pleases as I tremble with pleasure. My very being starts to unravel at the seams. When his lips reach my ear he nibbles on the lobe, then sucks it into his mouth, and my toes curl into the sand.

A low, primal growl hums from his chest as his body responds to mine. A whimper escapes my lips, and my hips urge me forward. Slowing his assault, he pulls back and whispers in a low and brooding voice, "I can't protect you, Alexis. Always remember what I truly am. One day I'll hurt you, and you'll wish you'd listened to me."

I wake up to a chill, trying to snuggle closer to the warmth that's been by me throughout the night, but it's gone. Rustling from across the room draws my consciousness from the darkness. I jerk up, and a thundering pain splits across the back of my skull.

"Shhhh, it's okay. I'm here." Jace's voice is like a blanket sliding over my body, warming everything from my toes to my ears.

He stayed all night. The thought beats in rhythm with the blood pounding inside my head.

I know it has to be early, as the room is barely lit with a soft glow. Squinting through my dim surroundings, I see a glass of ice water, two aspirin, a donut, and a cup of coffee. "Where did you get this stuff?"

Jace returns to the bed, and I notice he's dressed. He hands me the aspirin and then offers me the water. "Ann and Ty didn't get home until about thirty minutes ago. I had Ty bring them."

"Does Ann know you stayed the night?" If she knows Jace stayed, she'll ask questions, which means I'll have to tell her about my father.

He gives me a look. "You don't want her to know I stayed?"

"No, not really." He pulls away a bit, and I realize my mistake. "No, not that you stayed but the details of you staying—you caring for me, me getting drunk, why I got drunk." My gaze darts back and forth between his eyes, desperately wanting him to understand.

Jace furrows his brow. "So you're not going to talk to her about it?"

"No, I'm not." My head pounds. A foggy haze is settled over my thoughts, irritating me.

"You need to talk to someone about it. Death is natural; it happens to everyone eventually."

"Not helpful, and not your choice." I need time. I need to process how this is affecting me, and I cannot find the words to explain it to him, to make him understand without getting angry.

Jace growls, and despite the morbid conversation, my insides quiver at the sound.

"You are so stubborn. Why won't you talk to someone about it? You keep this bottled up and it can change you." His voice is pleading. It tugs at my soul.

"I just don't want to, okay? At least not right now."

"So you'll talk to someone eventually?"

"Yeah, eventually I will."

"Okay. Hey, listen." His large hand cups my cheek. "I have something I have to go take care of. I probably won't see you for a few days." While his eyes hone in on my lips, his thumb traces circles upon my skin. "I want to kiss you," he announces as he leans in, stopping a mere inch from my lips.

Memories from my dreams awaken my core, and I squirm under him. My patience breaks, and I push up, colliding into him with more force than I intended. His mouth molds over mine and pushes back into me. My hands tangle into his hair, pulling him into me with desire. When he breaks away we're both breathless. Our lips are swollen, and I can feel the firm pressure of his own desires on the back of my arm.

"I have to go now." And just like that, he's gone, leaving me with a frustration so deep my stomach hurts.

Chapter 17

Jace

The past few days have been hell, with the backlash from Marty after not answering his text and with my poor mental state since my night with Lexi. At the same time, things have become clearer. After I set things right with Marty, I did some investigating into Lexi's father's death. I contacted a few of my connections and found out he was involved with drugs. His dealers are part of an affiliate chapter to my club. He owed a lot of money to them, and when he couldn't pay up they killed him as a lesson to anyone else who might try to do the same. The feds have no idea who murdered him, and they never will unless they get intel from an inside source.

I realize right here and now if I want any sort of future with this woman, I have to get out as soon as possible. I find myself imagining what it would be like to be with her. I've never wanted anything so badly in my life. I have a plan—well,

I've been planning it for a while now, but she gave me a new reason. Now I know my choices before I met her were the right ones. It will be time to act upon them soon enough. First thing first, I need to talk to Lexi. I need to make sure she's doing okay mentally, that she talked to Ann.

Today she has only two classes, and I wait for her outside her last class. Leaning against the wall of the science building, I watch as people start filing out and search for her in the crowd. When I see Ann, I jog over.

"Hey, where's Lexi?"

Ann smiles at me like she knows some secret I don't. "She's been sick the past few days. She stayed home. Why, what's up?"

"Sick, huh? Thanks, Ann, I gotta go."

She calls after me, but I ignore her.

After parking my bike in front of the old farmhouse, I walk up to the door. My knocks go unanswered. I pull out my phone to call, only to remember I don't have her number yet. Then a noise echoes from the side of the house.

The grunts and huffs lead me to a rounded metal pen, where I catch a glimpse of how Lexi is dealing with her issues. She's on the back of a light tan horse, with a determined set to her shoulders. Both beast and beauty are drenched in sweat. The white tank top Lexi is wearing clings to her body, and the quick, jarring movements she's forcing the animal to do have me aroused before I even reach the fencing. I pull myself onto a panel as I take in her facial expression. A fixated focus pinches her brows together. She either didn't see me approach or is ignoring me.

The horse looks young but huge compared to Lexi's small frame. As the beast turns in a tight circle, Lexi moves the reins in her hands, and he quickly turns the other way. She then moves her hands back to the middle, and the horse stops, planting its feet. She clicks, and after no response from the animal she moves her feet into his sides. Nothing. She flips the ends of the leather reins over her hip, swatting him on the rump. He jerks his head from side to side and lowers it as though he's about to buck, but Lexi pulls the reins back, taking away his momentum, and he returns to his motionless position. At first he holds his ground, but then his front legs wobble slightly. He gives in, and his feet move them both forward. She walks him around the pen a few times, completely ignoring my presence, then dismounts at the far end after patting the horse's neck. Opening the gate, she walks him into the barn without so much as a glance back.

Chapter 18

Lexi

I walk Trigger back to his stall, telling him how well he did. Glancing over my shoulder, I see Jace following us, and I grin. He leans against the stall door as I start loosening Trigger's girth strap.

"Sick, huh?"

My grin fades.

"I'm just taking a swing in left field here, but I'm going to say you haven't talked to Ann?"

I lift the saddle and push past him. "That is none of your business."

"No matter how hard you try to push this away, it's real. It happened; death changes people. It's easier to understand that change by talking about it."

I emerge from the tack room. "Oh, and you're some expert on death?"

"No, I didn't say that, but when you see it happen enough, you learn how to deal with it."

I know he's trying to help, but I can't stop myself from lashing out at him. "My father died five years ago! He abandoned me because he got a new family! I've already grieved—I've already talked about it. I shouldn't have to do it twice! I didn't ask for your advice, so don't shove it down my throat."

I take a deep breath and continue. "You have quite the reputation for having lots of sex, yet you keep your distance from me. So before you try and help, you might want to reevaluate how much you really care about me." I stand my ground, facing him, daring him to argue. I'm breathing hard and completely surprised by those last words that fell from my mouth.

Jace's jaw clenches, and his eyes flare. I fully expect him to yell at me, to say something, anything. So when he turns to leave, I can do nothing but stand there gaping at him and regretting my words.

∞∞∞

That night I break down and tell Ann everything. At first she doesn't understand why I kept it from her, but she consoles me all the same.

"He was gone long before he actually died. The moment he found his new girlfriend, he wasn't the man I'd come to love. When he had his daughter, I lost him forever. He was my world, but his world became his new family. He let his girlfriend treat me like a piece of trash. She always asked him, 'How could you love something that isn't even yours?' She broke me mentally. She made me think I was undeserving of his love. I hated her so much. She took him away from me. The last time I saw him...I was thirteen. She called him home from work because my radio was up too loud. Instead of just coming in my room and telling me to turn it down...he kicked me out because I yelled at him, confused and hurt with the situation. That he was treating me so shitty because she didn't want me there. That was three weeks before Christmas." The anger that quickly built inside me at the memory takes me by surprise.

I glance at Ann, who wipes a tear from her eye. "Why didn't you tell me all this before? I knew he left you, but you never told me about his girlfriend."

"I-I was ashamed. I felt so weak by how she made me feel, how easily he gave up on me." Inhaling deeply, I continue. "I knew he loved me when he and Mom were together. He wasn't going to get the Father of the Year award or anything, but I still knew. For the longest time I always thought he would change back and come looking for me. I dreamed he would apologize and try to make amends. I wrote him only as much as my broken spirit could handle because he never wrote back. The feeling of rejection and abandonment changed me so much, so quickly.

"The cops are saying he was murdered, but they have no leads. He drove a water truck. They shot at his wheels, causing him to lose control and roll it. Then I guess he was crawling away and they shot him in the head." Ann's eyes widen. "Now I can stop waiting for a letter from him..." Ann breaks down and pulls me into a hug as she sobs into my hoodie.

After a moment she pulls away and apologizes. "You are so strong to be able to hold it all together right now." She sniffles.

I shrug. "I just don't understand. Why would someone want to murder him? Aside from being a shitty dad, he was a good guy. He got along with everyone. When I was a kid I remember Mom not wanting to take him shopping with her because he would talk to random people like they were old buddies." I smile at the memory.

Wiping her eyes with the sleeve of her sweater, she asks, "When is the funeral? Are we gonna go?"

Huddled together on the aging brown couch in the living room, we try to keep warm in front of the fireplace as a storm sputters outside.

"I want to, but I wouldn't be welcome. And besides, I already went through him being gone. I've done my mourning, going through all the steps—shock, anger, denial, then acceptance. I don't think I should have to do this twice..."

Ann nods, uncharacteristically at a loss for words.

"I have to apologize to Jace. I was awful to him today."

"Oh, sweets, you're being too hard on yourself. You needed to do things in your own time, and he was being pushy. I get why you lashed out." She takes my side in true best-friend fashion. "Although, I have to go by their house tomorrow to get something from Ty. If you want, you can come with."

"Okay, yeah, I'd like that."

Ann leans forward. "So, you and Jace?"

I smile. "I don't know. There is something between us—that's for sure—but I'm not certain what it is yet." I sigh, relieved to be able to talk about him. "He has a dark beauty to him; it's mesmerising. But he's so guarded, like anything he says might reveal that he's living a double life."

She smiles mischievously. "The Boston brothers have impeccable genes though."

I nod in agreement. "That they do. We haven't even slept together, yet I have never been so sexually aroused in my life."

"Really? No nookie?"

I shake my head. "You and Ty have, I'm guessing?"

"Actually, uh, no, we haven't." Ann looks away, and I don't press the issue given her recent trauma. I imagine Ty is a sort of safe space for her. He was there for her the night she was drugged. He must understand why she would be reluctant to be intimate without her having to explain anything.

"Do you think he hasn't tried because I'm giving him mixed signals?" I ask, taking the attention off her own romantic life.

"No, sweets, that's not what I meant... I mean, do you want to have sex with him?"

"Oh God, yes! I feel like a budding teenager with raging hormones when I'm around him." Simply saying it out loud makes my thighs tingle.

"Does he know you want to have sex?"

I try to recall each one of our encounters. "Honestly, I don't know."

Ann shrugs and tilts her head, giving me a smug look, like she's unlocked a riddle to find the treasure in an Indiana Jones movie.

∞∞∞

The next day as Ann drives us to Tyler and Jace's house, I pick at my nails, completely nervous about what I'm going to say to Jace. I need to apologize and give him the green light for the sex train.

"We're here," Ann announces, smiling at me with a knowing look.

I wipe my hands on my pants and reach for the handle of the car door, then pause, overcome by doubts.

"Lexi, if he really cares about you, he will understand why you lashed out at him."

I flip my visor down, checking my hair and the sparse makeup I applied to my face before leaving the house. "It's not the apology I'm nervous about."

"Oh. Well, the only way to not be nervous about the other thing is to just dive in, hop on, and drop them panties. Really, the amount of effort you'll have to put into that should be zilch." Ann mimics my primping as she pulls her hair to the side and quickly criss-crosses it into a perfect braid. I can't help but notice she's wearing less makeup than normal, and there's a glow to her that makes me smile as she exits the truck. At least one of us is doing well in the guy department. Walking up to me, she links arms with me, and we enter the house. Ann says, "Honey, I'm home" loudly from the foyer.

Ty greets us and pecks Ann on the cheek before ushering us into the kitchen, where another guy—Cooper, I assume—is sitting at a breakfast bar with his head in his hands. I smile at his apparent hangover as he murmurs something about shooting a death ray into the sun.

A girl stirring a pan full of delicious-smelling eggs says over her shoulder, "Hey! You guys hungry?"

"Diah, this is my best friend Lexi. Lexi, this is Cooper's girlfriend Diah, and yes, I would love some please."

Diah turns to Ann and me with a plate in her hand. "Hey, friend, nice to meet you. I actually think I know who you are." She deposits the plate in front of Ann, then steps back and puts her hands on her hips. "Well, not personally yet—but yeah, I think I've heard Jace mention you." Her eyes have an inviting warmth to them—almost like a grand-mother's eyes. They make you feel safe, but the girl can't be any older than I am. I instantly like her.

"Oh, all good things, I hope. And uh, no thanks on breakfast. It smells amazing though." I laugh, knowing that eating with such a nervous stomach is not a great idea.

"Yes, yes! All good, all good."

Cooper groans from his facedown position. "Diah, you might want to speak up. I don't think the people in France heard you."

"Ah, you are so sweet, you know that?" she says a bit more loudly, smiling when he groans. Then she pours him a glass of orange juice.

"You really need to stop being so happy in the mornings. It's ruining my well-established misery." He groans once more, lifting his head to sip the drink.

Diah hands out the remaining plates, giving me a muffin. I smile my thanks. I pick at it, grate-ful for the distraction. His presence calls to me even before he enters the kitchen. His frame fills the doorway, drawing my attention. Instantly our eyes lock. He freezes, and I can't help but smile at him. His damp hair hangs down across his fore-head. His bare chest still glistens from the shower it's apparent he just emerged from. His boxers peek at me from above grey sweatpants that hang perfectly from his hips. A small noise, unheard by the chatter around me, escapes my lips, and I know my face must be flushed.

"Good morning, Grumpy Gus. Here's your breakfast." Diah pushes a plate toward the open chair at the bar.

Jace remains motionless, his eyes boring into mine. Then a smaller female figure wraps her arms around him from behind. He moves forward a few paces, and the figure slips past him. A girl about my age reaches up and kisses him on the lips, says a quick goodbye to everyone, and then heads out a side door after grabbing a banana.

The hurt that slams into my chest knocks the breath out of me, and the room grows small. My vision begins to blur around the edges, like the oxygen is being sucked from the air around me. I push away from the bar and walk briskly toward the front door. The voice from behind me cuts a hole in my chest.

"Alexis, wait!"

Chapter 19

Jace

I slam my fist on the counter. "Cooper, go explain to her that was your bratty little sister and not some bird I just slept with!"

"Sorry, mate, you know I'm useless until about an hour after waking up with a hangover."

I hear the front door slam and take off after her, throwing various threats over my shoulder as I go.

Outside, Lexi is already down the drive and about to get into her truck.

"You have got to be kidding me!" I sprint toward her. "Lexi, wait!" I grab the door from her hand. "Will you just listen to me?"

She turns to me, a mixture of emotions swirling behind her eyes. "Hey"—she throws her hands up, avoiding my eyes—"I just came over here to apologize for the way I treated you yesterday. You didn't deserve that."

"Lexi—"

She jerks away from my touch, and frustration ignites in my stomach. "And I don't deserve this. I—"

Nope, gotta stop this now.

"Alexis! That girl in there, that wasn't what you think. She's Cooper's little sister who spent the summer in Italy, or some shit, and came back thinking it's cool to kiss everyone on the lips like that."

"Yeah, right—you sure pulled that lame story out of your ass quick."

Running a hand down my face, I growl. "Why would I lie to you when I know you could go inside right now and ask Ann? She's been here all week. She knows Missy."

Frustration and humiliation flash in her eyes as I reach out to her slowly. Knowing I'm playing with her pride, I gently pull her into my chest, and it takes her a moment to thaw.

"Why don't we go back inside? I believe there was something you wanted to apologize for?"

She pushes me away in mock annoyance. "If you're expecting anything more than what you just got, you haven't been paying attention." She purses her lips but can't hide the slight twitch of a grin, and I release a breath I didn't realize I was holding.

I lace our fingers together and pull her in the direction of the house. "I think it's best if we discuss this privately."

When I close my bedroom door I almost regret the decision. Lexi wanders around my empty room, her cheeks still tinged with pink. *What is she thinking?* Her behavior makes me feel vulnerable, and I shift my weight uneasily. After her evaluation is over, she turns her beautiful blue eyes on me. I look down at her.

"There actually is something else I wanted to talk to you about." She takes a deep breath and saunters forward. Something primal inside me stirs. "I may have been giving you mixed signals before, and I want to clear that up now." She's wearing a bit more makeup than usual, driving her exotic look to the next level. She pulls her tank top over her head in one tantalizingly smooth motion. My arousal grows to an almost painful level.

My eyes zero in when her hands move to the waistband of her jeans. I lick my lips in anticipation as she unbuttons them and they hang loose around her hips. "I hate to break it to you, but I'm not that type of man, Alexis Trucco."

My words bring a smile to her full lips, and something snaps within me. In one quick motion my arms are around her, lifting her. My lips are on her skin; I drink in her taste and inhale her scent. I know my motions are rough. I try to be gentle, but she answers my actions with a few rough love bites on my shoulder, and it sends me over the edge. The wall rushes up to meet us. When we collide with it, I hear something from the other side fall and shatter on the floor. A moan escapes her, vibrating her bare chest against my own, and the contact of her skin on mine ignites a fire within me that's so hot I fear it will burn us both.

I pull back. Her lips are swollen and wet as she gasps for breath. Her eyes look up to me from beneath dark lashes. A bewitching grin takes over her features as she raises a hand to finger the waistband of my sweatpants. My dick pushes hard against the grey fabric, eager for her attention. One of her hands slides inside, down across my pelvis with slow purpose. As her fingers wrap around my length, she sucks in a quick breath between her teeth.

My hands are on her, devouring her skin and exploring her curves. My finger slips under the strap of her bra, and I slide it down her shoulder. One beautifully awakened breast puckers as my breath comes down upon it. Taking her hardened bud into my mouth, I suck, then pull back to take it between my teeth. Her body pushes against mine with renewed need. I suck harder, and her grip on my dick tightens. My insides clench, and I flex in her hand. Her fingers find the moistened tip. I push back into her, my hand seeking the open front of her jeans. I so badly want to slip inside the cotton panties that lie against her beautiful skin, but I refrain, wanting to inflict as much pleasure upon her body as I can.

My hand glides over her, and she lifts herself onto her tiptoes with impatience. I smile into her neck when my fingers are greeted with a sweet dampness that calls to my baser instincts. I push into her, feeling her lips part, and move my fingers up and down against her slick center. Her body quivers against me, and she strokes my length in response. I quicken my motions as pleasure warms my body, and her head lolls back. A low, guttural sound rips from my chest, and I lift her again, causing us to break apart temporarily. Laying her across my bed, I settle over her as she entwines her legs around me, pulling me into her. Our kisses are softer, longer, pulling a sensation from me that I've never experienced before. I'm mildly aware that I'm not fighting the feelings. Instead I'm diving headfirst into the unknown abyss.

I drop kisses along her jaw, down her neck, and back up again.

A knock echoes in the background. I growl as I pull back slightly. "Go the fuck away!" Silence answers me as I slide my hand down her stomach and pull at her hips.

Three quick knocks—louder than before— have me pulling myself from her warmth and storming to the door. Jerking it open with all the force of my frustration, I say, "What!?"

Tyler stands before me, a serious expression on his face. Conflicting emotions swirl in his eyes. His voice comes out low, only meant for me to hear. "Marty just called. We have a problem."

Chapter 20

Lexi

I've tried so hard not to take the events of the past week personally, but I'm only human. My pride and pleasure are in a tailspin clawing at each other like free falling falcons. I don't know if it's because of my fear of how far things got that night with Jace or because of how far they didn't go. Either way, as the days have gone by with no word from him, I've begun to wonder if it was a good thing we didn't go all the way. When Ann tells me he contacted her, it rips my heart open.

"What did he want?" I ask, knowing my voice is betraying me.

"To make up for how he's acted this week." She searches my face.

"Make up for what? Being an asshole is in his nature." I shove my MMA gloves inside my gym bag, not looking at her.

It's been weeks since I've been to practice. With everything going on—from Ann being drugged to my father's passing—I've neglected my training. Getting back to the physical demands of practice will help everything become clear.

"Lexi, I think he really cares about you. It isn't just Jace who's gone AWOL. Ty has barely been around either."

I sigh as my curiosity begins taking control of the situation. "What exactly is his grand scheme to set things right?"

Ann smiles. "I can't tell you, but just know if I thought you wouldn't like it, I would tell you. Or if I felt this dude was being a total twat goblin, which I don't."

Clenching my jaw, I push open the door and head out of the house. From behind me Ann yells, "Love you!"

That night at practice a breath of cleansing air is pushed back into me. My legs quiver, and my arms are like lead. Sweat beads across my forehead, dripping down my face to my chest. I stare at Nick, his glistening chest rising with each labored breath. We've been sparring for the past ten minutes, and I'm exhausted but exhilarated. As his body begins to move, my eyes follow. He's circling me, so I prepare for an attack and watch for an opening. All my stress, all my turmoil melts away.

I'm forced to focus or be punched in the face. My mask is stripped away, and I'm left with nothing but instinct and the drive to never give up.

Nick's demeanor toward me is guarded, but not rudely so. His eyes rake over me as I mirror his movements. A quick flurry of jabs causes me to cover up and take a few steps back. He shoots in for a takedown, and my body responds accordingly, causing him to miss. Dropping down, my chest crushes into his back as I try to flatten him out.

He pushes up.

I swivel my body behind him, raining punches down on each side of his head.

He has no choice but to guard his face. He stands and bounces away from me, smiling.

I must have hurt him with one of my blows.

He raises his hands and starts back after me.

This time, however, I push the pace, bouncing around to make him chase me. Every so often he takes a deep breath, and in doing so, his hands drop slightly.

My stomach tightens with anticipation as I bait him forward.

He breathes deeply.

I shift my hips and twist my body so my dominant leg can arch through the air.

I normally don't try head kicks, as my legs are short and I lack confidence, but tonight I simply feel it come together when the opportunity presents itself. Moments before my shin reaches

Nick's head I pull back some of my power, not wanting to actually hurt him. When it lands, I hear the impact as much as I feel it.

Nick's hands drop to his sides, and he stumbles backward.

As soon as my foot returns to the ground I rush forward to check on him. "Oh my God, are you okay? I am so sorry. I didn't think that I would actually catch you with that."

He blinks a few times, then erupts in laughter.

I put my hand on his shoulder, half worried I knocked a few screws loose. Then his laugh infects me, and I start laughing too.

"You fucking got me good." He brings his hand to his head, and I turn his face toward me to look at it.

Upon some swelling I try to control myself as I say, "You are so going to get a black eye from that." Nick looks at me, and we both burst out laughing again. Coach calls an end to the class, and I take a steadying breath, enjoying the much needed release.

Pulling off his gloves, Nick says, "I'm really glad you're back. I wanted to come see you after I heard what happened with your dad, but I figured Jace wouldn't be too happy about it."

"What? Why would you care what he thinks?"

Nick tilts his head as he watches me. "Aren't you two together now?"

I laugh as the bitterness I have toward Jace laces its way into my words. "Uh, no, we are not together."

He nods, lowering his voice marginally as people pass us heading for the locker rooms. "When you told me you weren't interested in me I figured he was a part of your reasoning."

My stomach churns, and a horrible heart-ache stirs in my chest as I realize how I must have made him feel.

He pulls his brows together at whatever it is he sees on my face. "Hey, don't. Don't do that. Don't look at me like that. I'm fine. I get it. I'm cool with just being your friend. Although, I am glad to hear you're not seeing him. You are way too good for him."

"You're sweet, but I'm no angel myself." I pull off my gloves and start to unwrap my hands.

"No, maybe not." Nick rubs his head where I kicked him. "But you're smart and beautiful and one of the most driven and capable women I've ever known."

I throw my glove at him, and he dodges it.

"And you're kind of a little shit."

I pick up my other glove and throw it.

He puts his hands up, laughing. "Hey, wait, um...so is it okay if I come to your birthday party this weekend then?"

My birthday? I didn't even realize it was ap-proaching.

Nick notices my confused look and follows

up with, "Ann gave everyone here an invite last weekend. It didn't say it was a surprise party, so I hope I didn't just mess things up…"

I shake my head. "Uh, yes. I mean, no. Yes, you can come, and no… You didn't mess anything up."

Nick grins his beautiful grin. "Okay, cool. See you then."

I return the smile and turn to leave, fully intent on berating Ann when I get home.

Chapter 21

Jace

This week has been one of the hardest weeks of my life. I have hurt people, put my life in danger, and betrayed old friends. Isolating Tyler has been the hardest, but I can't let him get involved. Having him pissed at me has made it easier to follow through with things. Even before Will got locked up and Scott took off, Tyler was always the one I told everything to. Everything except how I truly feel about the club. He's seen me in my darkest moments, and keeping my enlistment from him has been tough. Marty has been the most difficult to deal with after the truth came out, but once I pointed out that the training I would receive as a Marine would only help me in my position as his enforcer, he got off my back—at least, long enough for me to get the information I needed from a few of the members.

I know he'll retaliate; it's only a matter of time. I have everything lined out, and it all begins with the party tonight. I need to say goodbye to Lexi. I don't want to hurt her any more than I already have, but I want at least one person in this world to see some good in me. If she's the only one to remember me as a decent human being, it will all be worth it.

Tomorrow I'll be on my way to repay the man who killed Lexi's father. If her birthday present tonight isn't enough, maybe offering her some sort of justice will be.

Chapter 22

Lexi

Ann strung twinkling lights from one end of the backyard to the other. She has my playlist playing, she prepared my favorite food—taco salad—and the yard is full of people who I could honestly do without. The stocked bar that Tyler brought is making up for it though. I dance and drink and eat until my heart is content. My mom even calls to wish me a happy birthday.

So when Nick asks me to dance, I don't have the heart to say no. Thankfully he keeps his hands to himself, and the fast-paced music drives our crazy dancing. He does the robot, and I laugh, trying to mimic him. Another song passes as we kick our legs and wave our hands. I'm thankful he still wants to be friends. I've grown to adore him. Then the song switches to a slow, even beat that dictates everyone's moves for them.

I look away awkwardly. "Hey, I uh, I'm going to go to the restroom. I'll be back shortly."

The slow melody drifts through the screen door, filling the house with a magical energy. My skin peppers with gooseflesh. I wet my face in the kitchen sink, using the hand towel to wipe away the water and sweat. I turn to head upstairs, and a shadow leaning against the doorframe catches my attention.

He regards me with dark eyes, emotions hidden by the lack of light. My stomach grows tight as my gaze roams his body. "If you think some birthday present will make up for you being a total dick, then you are sadly mistaken."

Jace pushes forward out of the darkness, tilting his head to the side. "Damn, you called my hand, Ace." The glow from the lights outside filters into the kitchen window, blanketing everything in a soft light. The slow song is still playing in the background. "Dance with me?"

I scoff. "You know how to dance?"

Jace rubs the back of his neck with one hand while the other pushes further into the pocket of his jeans. "Uh, no. No, I don't, but it's slow dancing. How hard could it be?"

I quickly remind myself what happens when our bodies get anywhere near each other. "Ya know, I think I'ma have to pass. Ann is waiting for me out back." I turn to go, but his large hand wraps around my wrist with a gentle grip.

"Please, don't go."

"Can you just fuck off already?" I turn back to him, intending to rip my hand from his grasp, but the rawness within his eyes causes my breath to catch in my throat.

He lets go, growling under his breath. "What more do you want from me? I have no idea how to do this stuff, okay? I—" He steps away and runs a hand through his hair, then breathes deeply before turning back to me. His eyes awaken a heat within me while he speaks. "Alexis, I am so sorry that I haven't been around. I wish I could tell you some brilliant line to make you understand the importance of what I was doing, but I can't. I just want you to know that I am truly, deeply sorry for any pain I may have caused you."

He cannot take away the pain he's caused by blowing me off all week, but part of me wants to make him try. A more stable side of me knows that I'm the only one in control of my mental state. I can choose to stay mad at him, snuff out any chance we may have at a relationship, or I can forgive him. "The slow song is over," I say as I take a step toward him.

He tilts his head to the side, watching me for a moment, then takes a step of his own. "I don't know, I kinda thought we moved to a beat of our own." He lifts a hand, and I intertwine my fingers with his as he pulls me close to him with the other. The tightness in my stomach spreads throughout my body. We press into each other and sway to an unheard rhythm.

"Happy Birthday," he whispers as his lips rest on my forehead.

Smiling, I curl into him, savoring this moment, committing it to memory. A cough from behind causes me to glance over my shoulder, where I see Nick. He has one hand on the door, his body angled away from us. The hurt is blatantly evident in his eyes.

"Uh, Ann is looking for you. She said it's time to cut the cake." Even though he looks defeated, his eyes meet Jace's, and the tension is palpable in the air.

I pull out of Jace's arms, but he doesn't let go of my hand. "Oh, okay. Well, lead the way then."

I pull Jace outside, and he grunts behind me, causing me to smile again. Outside, everyone is gathered around a table. They split apart to allow me to pass.

Dropping my hand, Jace hangs back in the crowd.

The cake before me is huge, with the words "Last Year as a Teen" written across it in icing. Ann beams at me, starting the customary birthday song. I duck my head to blow out the nineteen candles.

Present opening is next. I sigh at the box Ann extends out to me. I hate gifts. Despite that it's my birthday and gifts are customary, I don't like feeling obligated to the gift givers. It's too much pressure. I force a smile and open the box. Inside is a beautiful pair of cowboy boots. They're a deep brown with purple stitching. These had to cost her a fortune.

"Ann, you—"

"Oh hush, don't say a word about the price. I made a few connections around town with some top-of-the-line designers and got them dirt cheap." I purse my lips at her ability to read my mind.

Nick steps up, sighing deeply as he hands me a box. I try to fill my "Thank you" with all the remorse I feel about the whole situation.

He waves me off, and inside the box I find a pair of MMA gloves. Not knowing what to say, and feeling like I just want to get the fuck out of here, I simply offer him a smile.

Last, I pick up a small box wrapped in plain brown paper with a purple bow on top. Inside I find a note that says: *Turn around.*

Behind me stands Jace. Next to him is Trigger, who is fully decked out in brand-new matching tack. Upon his back is a stunning saddle with the same colors and stitching as my boots. He dons a matching bridle, which I can't help but notice is buckled incorrectly. I quickly fix the buckle and briefly wonder who got him ready.

"Was this you?" I ask Jace.

"Sorta. Ann helped pick out the colors to make sure they matched her present." He smiles, handing me Trigger's reins. "Try it out."

Ann rushes up beside me. "Oh, but wait. Put these on first." She hands me the boots.

"You guys, this is too much," I say, despite my excitement to try out the new gear. As I pull

myself into the smooth new saddle, I see Jace leading a saddled Kashi up next to us.

I look at Jace. "You're going to ride Kashi?" I
know the old man is an easy ride for any beginner,
but it's dark.

"I've done a little riding in my day." I knit
my brows. There isn't much I actually know about
this man.

"Oh, is that so?"Adrenaline pours into my
veins, and a crazy-lady grin splits my face. With
a few clicks, Trigger immediately responds under
me. He rockets across the yard and out into the
pasture. His gait is smooth, and his strides have us
across the ten acres of clear land before I can look
to see if Jace is following. As the tree line forms
before us, I slow him. My head lifts into the clouds
with how well he's responding to commands.

Behind us, a silhouette of a beautiful, mys-
terious man upon a horse moves in the moonlight.
When they draw nearer, Jace pulls Kashi up, slowing him down. I marvel at his obvious experience.

"Where did you learn to ride like that?" I ask
when he comes closer.

Falling in beside me, he says, "We have a
mountain cabin. We used to go up to it every
summer when I was a kid. Marty, my mother's
boyfriend, had a lot of friends that would bring
up their young horses to have them broken. They
thought it would be funny to put an eight-year-old
kid on a greenie. Everyone was surprised when I
hung on. Well.. at least, longer than they were ex-

pecting."

I shake my head, trying to imagine what Jace looked like as a young boy. "They sound like a great batch of parentals."

He looks away. "I don't wanna talk about me anymore. I have something to show you." He passes me on Kashi, pushing into the woods and down the trail that leads to the river. I click a few times, and Trigger tries to take off under me. I give him a few directions, and he falls into a nice walk with minimal sass.

After a few moments Jace gets off Kashi, leading him off the trail. I follow, fully intrigued by the situation. Then, as I'm about to ask what we're doing, a glow ahead of us draws my attention. Getting closer, I see it's some sort of tee-pee covered in white semi-transparent cloth with the same twinkling lights from the party draped around it. I look at Jace while he ties Kashi to a tree. He winks at me, and my insides clench with anticipation. I quickly tie Trigger up and walk closer.

Inside, the ground is covered in a thick white blanket with a border of sunflowers.

"My favorite flower?" I feel like I could levitate off the ground. He's being exceptionally sweet, and I like it. There's something about the chemistry between us that I have a deep desire to explore.

He shrugs. "I gave Ann a gift card for the spa for all her help."

"So you're essentially telling me what you have planned tonight will be better than a full day at the spa?" I flash him a teasing smile. He walks closer, his eyes roaming my body.

"I don't know what kind of spas you've been to, but yes, this night will be one you will remember for years to come."

I narrow my eyes at him. "You are such an egotistical ass." My smile turns into a smirk as I try to ignore the charge floating all around us.

He laughs. "Come on, I have something for you." He pulls me into the makeshift tent, and we sit on the fluffy blanket. Jace reaches around a wooden crate in back and pulls out a small box topped with a silver bow.

"Another present?" I eye him hesitantly as I take it, a retort on the tip of my tongue.

"Yes, except this one was all me. No Ann." Smiling at the proud look on his face, I remove the bow and lift the lid. Inside lies a necklace on a thin silver chain. Attached to it is a small glass vial. Inside the vial are black and grey metallic flakes.

I'm not a fan of traditional jewelry. I don't even own any aside from a few old earrings, but there is something about this piece that calls to me. "Jace, this is absolutely stunning. Is that metal?"

He nods. "From the ring we fought in the night we met."

I whip my head around. His eyes search mine. "What? How did you get this? How did you not get arrested for getting this?" I am concerned for his lack of personal safety, but I can't help it when a wide grin stretches across my face.

"You like it?" he asks, avoiding my question.

"There is something raw about it," I admit as I look at it again, remembering that night.

"So...?"

Laughing, I give him the answer he's looking for. "Yes, I do. Will you put it on me?"

Nodding, he scoots closer, grazing my neck with his fingertips when he fastens the clasp. My body ignites with a tingling sensation so strong I almost feel numb. Then he scoots back to look at me, and the feeling fades marginally.

"Yikes," he says, and my eyes shoot to him. His brow furrows, and he appears conflicted.

"What? What is it?" I look down, thinking I've somehow broken it already.

"I don't know what I was thinking... That is a horrible gift. Here, give it back and I'll get you something better."

I lean away, wrapping a protective hand around the vial when he reaches for the necklace. "No—no take backs."

Jace pulls up on his knee. "I'm being serious. Give it to me." He reaches out again.

"No!" I turn to try and crawl out of the tent, but he grabs my waist, pinning me down. I shift my hips to create space between us. As he comes down on top of me, I wrap him up with my legs, placing him in my guard. I push my hips away when he reaches again, but this time his hands snake around my middle, pulling me onto him. Sitting on his lap, I pull the necklace away with one hand and push on his chest with the other.

My breath grows labored with the effort. I smile with triumph when he doesn't attempt to grab it. My arm relaxes as my eyes wander his face. His lips are parted slightly, hot breath whispering out onto my chest. I'm suddenly oh-so aware of how close we are. My gaze softens, and the intensity in Jace's eyes causes my brain to freeze for a heartbeat. Then before my cognitive ability returns to me, my lips are crashing into his. His hands flatten on the small of my back for a moment before they work their way up, rounding over my shoulders with firm resolve. My lungs scream for air, but my core moistens with need. So when Jace turns his head to kiss my neck, I inhale deeply. My mind grows dizzy from the sudden pull of oxygen—or perhaps it's his scent. Either way, I know what I want, and I slip my hands under his shirt, feeling his hard muscles pulsing beneath my fingertips. I lift his shirt, tossing it to the side, where my own shirt quickly joins it. My sports bra follows suit. As soon as my breasts are free, Jace takes one into his mouth.

My body arcs with pleasure, filling me with desire. Pushing him onto his back, I rain kisses down on his chest. My breast puckers, a chill gracing the damp spot his beautiful lips left behind. My body breaks out in a shiver, and Jace pushes me away slightly. "Are you cold?"

A reverberating moan rips from my chest. "Will you shut up and just fuck me already!"

Something feral blazes in his eyes, and he scoops me up, drawing me beneath him, and settles on top of me. Our hips come together, and his hardness presses into my center. My legs tremble, eager for the barrier between us to vanish. He pulls away, undoing my pants while kissing across my chest and down to my stomach. As he reaches my pelvis, I buck into him, giving him the space needed to pull off my jeans. My panties slide down with them, and in one quick motion I lie before him, naked except for my emotions. His eyes rake over me and consume me. My legs itch to pull him back in, but he dips his head and scoots back.

When the warmth of his tongue hits my skin, my hands knead the blanket and my toes curl. With a tantalizing slowness he flicks his tongue back and forth, making me twitch with each pass. His assault continues for uncounted minutes, and when he pulls away I'm eager to have him inside me. My core clenches, already nearing my peak.

When he settles over me, I'm wound so tightly that my legs are shaking. His hardened warmth meets my center, stopping with tantalizing anticipation. "Do I need a condom?" His voice is low and raw. His eyes search mine.

I stare at him blankly before I comprehend that he is waiting for a response. "No, no—I'm on birth control," I state, irritated that we didn't have that conversation beforehand.

Sliding forward, he sheathes himself to the root in one stroke, stretching me with indescribable pleasure. A sound of ecstasy escapes my lips. My core tingles and clenches as he sits unmoving. Then slowly he pulls back. My eyes flutter, and my head tips back. Jace leans down, peppering me with soft kisses as he sinks back into me with more force. Our lips find each other, and I take his tongue between my teeth, trying to convey what I want. At the same time, my fingers rake across his back, pulling him down.

Something about Jace's moan sings to my internal sex goddess, and my hips rush up to meet his quickened thrusts. I bite my lip, and his hand curls around my jaw. His thumb commands the attention of the swollen flesh. Dragging his thick appendage across it, I take it into my mouth, sucking. Again his pace quickens. There is no beginning or end to my building response.

His eyes dance in mine before I arch up, quivering, holding my breath until my mind goes blissfully blank.

Chapter 23

Jace

To say I'm experiencing internal conflict would be a huge fucking understatement. Throughout my life I've always known who I am, *what* I am, and accepted it. But when the sun begins to shine through the trees, taking some of the chill from the early morning, I want nothing more than to be someone else, to not have the issues and problems that come with living my life. As I pull from Lexi's warmth I damn my life to hell and back. When her eyes open and she watches me get ready to leave, I hate the trust I see in their blue depths. She has no questions, no concerns, no idea of what I really am. Disgusted betrayal digs into my gut, even as my chest constricts my breathing.

Her short hair sticks out in all different directions, her features soft from sleep. The blankets she's buried under move with each breath she takes, mesmerizing me. The only thing that keeps me from crawling back to her is knowing I'm not good enough for her. My life, my past—hell, even my present—is something I hope she never has to know about.

I have no idea what her future holds, but I know whoever she ends up with will be one lucky bastard. I lean down to give her a final kiss, and the action almost breaks me. Crazy schemes swirl through my head like a tornado as I try to figure out a way to escape my life and still be with her. But I draw a blank. I've already considered all the options, and none of them are good enough for her. The goodbye catches in my throat, and I leave without saying a word.

The concept of time completely leaves me on the ride back to the barn, but the sun is threatening to peek around the mountains by the time I lead Kashi back into his stall and retrieve my Harley. The bike roars between my thighs, almost like my anger and disappointment are fueling it. I accelerate down the highway, surpassing the speed limit by double in a matter of seconds. As the hours tick by and my destination grows near, I wonder if Tyler has given her my letter. Saying goodbye to him was difficult. The day before yesterday I told him about my plan to leave, about how I need time to myself before I'm due to report for boot camp. He so kindly pointed out that I will have plenty of time alone in a week, and after a brief argument he agreed not to tell Lexi, or Ann for that matter. Although he didn't explicitly agree to give her my letter, I know I can count on him to do so anyway.

I picture her anger when she reads it, and I can see the pain reflected in her eyes. She will feel like I've played on her emotions. Ultimately, I hope she understands that I suck at saying good-bye. I hope our night together will be enough for her to understand how I feel about her. I hope she will remember that through the hate that will un-doubtedly consume her. I hope she is eventually able to move on, to be happy.

I know our affiliate club has heard I've been asking about the death of Lexi's father. They don't know why, but I realize I can't simply show up at their club. It would set them on edge, and that could quickly become a very fucked-up situation. Instead I check into a shitty hotel on the edge of town, making sure not to wear my patches, know-ing the place could be under the club's protection. Now all that's left to do is wait.

Chapter 24

Lexi

C onfusion is the dominant emotion in me when Tyler calls me that afternoon asking if I'll come by as soon as I get an opportunity. He tells me not to bring Ann or say anything to her. I wonder if, after what Jace did for me, Tyler wants to do something similar. Ann's birthday is only a few weeks after mine. I want to believe that's what it is, but something in his voice hints that isn't it at all.

My afternoon is blessedly empty, so after I take care of the livestock, I half limp upstairs to shower. My whole body aches from the previous night's events. The memory of how Jace's body consumed mine over and over again makes it hard to concentrate, and I end up spending twice the amount of time washing. After drying my hair, I flip open my phone to let Jace know I'm about to head over, but it goes straight to voicemail. It's the first time I've tried to call him, so I'm not sure what his phone habits are. I try to not let it get to me, but something gnaws at the inside of my stomach like I've swallowed a rat and it's trying to fight its way out.

Half an hour later when I pull up to their house, my heart sinks a bit when I don't see Jace's motorcycle. I knead the truck's keys between my fingers while I wait for someone to answer the door. The door swings in, and I hold my breath, releasing it with a small sigh when Diah's dainty face appears. She avoids making eye contact. My brows pull together at the action.

"Alexis."

The formal way my name slips from her lips has me rounding my shoulders back in defense. I don't remember doing anything wrong, but she's obviously upset.

"Diah, are you okay?" I ask, feeling like I'm missing some vital bit of information.

She turns and swipes a hand across her face, like she's wiping tears away. "Tyler is in the kitchen," she mumbles, darting off ahead of me. I want to comfort her, ask her if something happened between her and Cooper, but she leaves me little time to do so.

Walking into the kitchen, I immediately feel something is amiss. Tyler is on the phone and holds his finger up to me, then walks back into the pantry to finish his conversation. I sit down, trying to calm my nerves, but can't refrain from picking at my nails as different bizarre scenarios run through my head.

"You!" The voice behind me is cold and accusing. I turn to see Cooper blazing into the kitchen, a fiery light in his eyes.

Instinct pushes me to my feet as he approaches.

"This is all your fault!" A potent musk assaults my nostrils as he invades my personal space. *He's drunk.* His words tear apart my insides. I pull my right foot back, readying myself for whatever it is he assumes is my fault. "Ever since *you* started coming around, things have gotten all fucked up! You made Jace start questioning who he is. Who he was *born* to be! You have his head all twisted, and he is about to throw his life away for some little sadist whore!"

My fists clench, nails digging into my hands. His words leave lacerations across my heart and a deep pain in my chest. I begin to raise a fist, but a hand slips around my wrist, stopping the action. I turn, half expecting it to be Jace, but Tyler's softer features greet me instead.

He gently pulls me behind him. "Coop, you need to back off right now." His voice is a low rumble "She had nothing to do with Jace's decision. I doubt she even knows." His eyes are strikingly similar to Jace's. The confusion turns into anxiety and becomes unbearable. My body itches. *Flight or fight, Lexi.*

I pull away from Ty's grasp and step back around him, turning my face to his. "C-can you, or someone, *anyone*, please tell me what the hell is going on? Where is Jace? Why is everyone acting so..." My voice trails off and I shrug, helpless.

Tyler guides me over to a barstool and sits next to me. He takes a deep breath, and something in his expression changes, hardens. His gaze never leaves my own, and though I see pity in it, I also see terror. "I'm...so sorry, Lex. That you have to hear this, that this is reality." Then he explains that my father, Paul, was a drug peddler for a biker club in his town. The club is an extended chapter to the one that Jace, Ty, and Cooper are all in. My father started off doing well, bringing in lots of money for the club. He used his semi as a cover, filling it with drugs and delivering them to various buyers. Then he started using his product. He had no self control as he blew through the supply the club gave him. He owed them a large debt, which he ultimately paid back with his life.

Ty's words wash over me like a tsunami. Tears spill over my lashes, but my body is refusing to function, even to do something as miniscule as wiping away the tears. My chest rises and falls in small pants. I can't inhale to catch my breath for fear of sucking in a great gulp of the disastrous waters that are drowning me. Dizziness rocks my body, causing my head to spin. Slowly I piece it all together, making sense of the story.

Ty goes on to explain that by club law, the person who killed my father had every right to do so. My father was in the wrong, and the club, the *gang—Jace's gang*—was entirely in the right. I sit there dumbfounded, frozen, and he can do nothing but watch me with apologetic eyes. He raises a hand and places it on my shoulder, trying to comfort me. Except it does the opposite. Ever so slowly, fear and disbelief make way for the anger that was just beneath the shock. It snakes its way through my veins, making my body go red hot within seconds.

I feel betrayed.

I feel stupid.

Jace is...in a fucking *gang*.

Suddenly, Nick's words the night Jace and I met surface in my mind.

"Every time he is on a fight card all his biker buddies show up and start shit..."

Ann asked if that was like a gang, and Nick all but confirmed it.

I always assumed it was like some sort of car club, but with motorcycles. Nothing had ever hinted at—

The night we were at the club...it got shut down because of a fight. They later said it was because of some biker gang. Jace and Tyler were both there that night.

Ty continues spilling out his truth, not moving that fucking hand that is burning through the thin layer of cloth on my shoulder. "The person who killed your father was the enforcer of that club. Lexi, I...he... That position is the exact position Jace has in our club."

Tyler pauses, allowing his words to sink in. I stand, pulling away from his touch.

"Jace is on his way now to even the score. He is going to kill your father's killer, Lexi. If he succeeds, he will have broken club law. That's an immediate death sentence. Everyone in the club will be gunning for him. Even us." He motions to himself and Cooper, who is taking swigs from an almost empty bottle of Jack. "Well, obviously we won't go after him, not in that way anyway, but we'll be expected to."

I want to run. I want to get away from these masks before me. I feel so...so...I don't know what I feel. Powerless? Indignant? Righteously angry? My emotions are below the surface of a muddied pond. I can feel them, but I can't distinguish them from one another.

"Here." Ty nudges me, holding a slip of paper between his fingers. Deceptive fingers, murderous fingers. "Jace left this for you. It won't help explain things. He most likely never intended to tell you any of this."

I don't know how long I stand there staring at the paper before I actually reach out and take it. The words written down don't connect in my brain; they only confuse me more. I finally have to sit down on the barstool and take a deep breath. "The Marines?" My voice comes out in a whisper.

Tyler takes the paper from my hand and reads it. "Shit, I keep forgetting about that. He enlisted in the Marines too. He's going to be pissed when he knows I dragged you into this. This makes it clear." He hands me back the letter and begins to pace the living room. "He wanted you to think he was on his way to Basic."

"But..." I manage despite the lump in my throat. "Will he even make it to Basic? I mean, if he goes after the...the guy. The club guy."

"There's no if, Lexi. He is probably halfway there by now. When Jace makes his mind up... there's no stopping him. And the answer is no, at least from logic's standpoint. If he gets that far, he will die one way or another. He seems to think he'll make it, but he won't."

I can't breathe. My head spins. My vision tunnels.

Diah speaks up, her gaze never drifting my way. "We have to try to stop him. If we can intervene, maybe Marty will just rough him up a bit." Her voice is pleading, desperate.

My stomach rolls, threatening to empty onto the nice, clean tile.

"If anyone lays a finger on Jace, it will undo him. He'll lose any remaining respect for the club, and then he'll be as good as dead. We only have one option." Ty grabs his keys from the counter and stares me full in the face. "We have to stop him from killing this guy. I don't care about the backlash it might cause me with the club. As long as Jace gets out, it will be worth it. I know this is a lot to process, and I don't even know if I have the right to ask it of you, but will you come? Maybe seeing you will stop him."

Cooper splutters from behind me. "You are fucking nuts, Ty. If you do this, you lose your chance to become President." His face hardens, eyes darting between us.

In all the time I've known him, I've never seen Tyler lose his cool. He's always been sophisticated in the way he speaks, like he's always one step ahead of everyone, like he knows what's coming next. But not more than a second after the words leave Cooper's mouth, he erupts.

"What the fuck is wrong with you? He is my brother! What the fuck do you expect me to do? Am I to sit here while he ruins his life, while he puts a bullseye on his chest? For what? A position in a club? You are supposed to be his best friend. Aren't you going to try and save his life?"

Cooper's hesitation knocks the wind from my chest. "Get the fuck out of this house now!" Ty screams, stepping forward.

Cooper stays where he is, seemingly conflicted, then finally turns to leave. After a step, he stops and turns to face me. Before he can even say a word, Tyler is between us, shaking in anger. "So help me, Cooper, if you try to lay a finger on her or even *look* at her like that again, I will throw your body into a shallow grave without a second thought."

Cooper's eyes lock with Ty's. He grits his teeth and pulls his lips back in a snarl. "Diah, let's go!" The girl stays put, and Cooper rounds on her.

"NOW!"

She doesn't move. He takes half a step toward her, then changes his mind and storms out of the house, slamming the door so hard the windows rattle.

After a few moments, Diah turns to Tyler. "We need to talk." She glances at me for the first time today. "Alone."

When they go into the other room, I'm left with my thoughts, with the fresh knowledge about my father and the events surrounding his death. He died because he was dealing drugs... doing drugs. He chose to be a part of some gang, and ultimately that's what killed him. And Jace... Jace is going to avenge him. To...kill his murderer.

∞∞∞

When they resurface from the room a few moments later, we leave. Ty has no leads, and he can't risk asking any of the locals for fear it will tip the club off and put Jace in even more danger. Ty and I drive in silence for a while, consumed with our own thoughts. I think I doze off once or twice, but I can't be sure. I pay no attention to our surroundings, but when we pass under a large rusty arch, I know exactly where we're headed.

Memories flood into me, threatening to push me back over the edge. This is the town I spent two summers in as a young teen. The town I was abandoned in. How did we reach it so quickly? This is the road that I walked down years ago, armed with only a backpack full of clothes and a pocketknife. This is the cemetery I sprinted past, trying to escape the pain of him kicking me out. Now, he lies rotting in a grave somewhere among the thousands, no longer able to torment me by withholding his love, no longer able to do much of anything besides feed the worms.

"Why did you bring me here?" I ask as I stare out the window, watching the headstones drift past.

Ty sighs, a deep noise that doesn't come close to portraying the weariness I see etched in his face. "In a long line of fucked-upness, in some distant way his death is my fault too."

"No one forced him to do drugs. No one forced him to sell them."

Ty says nothing. He takes a right, passes two rows, then turns left.

"Do you know where he's buried?"

I sense rather than see him shake his head. "Just looking for a fresh grave."

The thought unsettles me. The need to escape overwhelms the logical part of my brain, and I open the door, ready to jump out. Ty slams on the brakes but remains silent.

The graveyard is...nice, I suppose. I'm not so sure what exactly is considered a nice place to be buried. But there is a fence...two arched gates... statues in memory of fallen soldiers... Alongside most of the graves are flowers or other tokens from loved ones.

I wander for who knows how long, reading but not really taking in the names around me. From the corner of my vision, I catch sight of a well-worn pair of workboots. The air is pulled from my lungs, and I stumble, leaning against a stranger's headstone. The familiarity of the scuffed leather pulls me forward, singing to me. My legs move of their own accord. Rounding on the hard, cold stone, I read the name next to the boots.

"Here Lies Luke Trucco."

"Oh God." My legs buckle under me, and I crash down, doubling over with wracking sobs. "Why! Why wasn't I enough? Why didn't you love me!"

My words get lost between the tears and snot that drip down my face, leaving soft impressions in the earth.

My fingers claw into the overturned dirt, bits of debris shifting under my nails.

My screams mix with the stillness of the fresh air, tainting it, dirtying it.

Minutes, hours, days, or perhaps only a few seconds pass as I slouch against the pristine headstone that spells out my daddy's name. Blindly I reach out, searching around for the dusty leather of his old boots. I find them and run a few fingers across them, feeling the pockmarks and creases, the life they once held. It's hard to comprehend that the man I once loved more than anyone is six feet beneath me.

Finally, albeit slowly, I pull myself from the shards of reality and sit up. My face is sticky and stiff, and my nails are caked with dirt and dried blood. I close my eyes, trying to remember my dad's laugh. It's been so long since I've heard it. I search the recesses of my mind for the way his pillow smelled, the thickness of his hair, the roughness of his hands, fingers cracked so badly they bled.

Senses dulled by grief, I don't immediately register the feral growl echoing behind me.

"You! You little bitch!" I flinch at the shrill voice, cowering closer to the cold stone. I don't need to glance over my shoulder to know who this woman is, the bane of my childhood existence. Her voice still haunts me, the high tones and mocking anger. This woman was supposed to make Daddy whole, supposed to give his life meaning, supposed to love me like her own child. Instead, she sentenced him to purgatory and me to a lifetime of hurt and distrust.

"What are you doing here? Have you not done enough, Alexis?"

Her voice and her words send me back in time. Suddenly, I'm a scared thirteen-year-old again, trembling before her. I manage a few feeble words before she cuts me off. "I-I only wanted to —"

" Only wanted to what? What exactly is it

that you think talking to a dead man will do for you, you fool!"

The venom in her words jolts me into action. I stand to flee but stumble over my own feet and trip, flying straight back into a warm body. I tense and prepare to fight my way out, but the body belongs to Tyler. Somehow, he is able to reassure me with only a look. He pulls me closer to him, enveloping me into his heat. Briefly, I wonder if he, too, can see the monster that stands in front of us, the one hiding behind a bad dye job and too-pink lipstick.

My recently widowed stepmother gasps, a hand flying to her mouth. "How dare you bring your trash here! I always said you were nothing but a little slut!"

Still, after all these years, I have no retort for her, no words of defense. Ty stiffens at her words, and his chest contracts with a deep breath.

"You have no right to be here. This is all your fault!" She advances toward us, a crazed look on her face. "If it wasn't for you, his daughter"—she points to the grave, eyes glowing—"his *true* daughter wouldn't be fatherless right now!"

But...nothing could be further from the truth. His death had nothing to do with me. I frown, turning my face from Ty's chest. "You're wrong. I haven't talked to him in years."

"You caused this! He couldn't let go of you, the weak man. He felt nothing but obligation for your worthless hide. When he tried writing you, I was disgusted! I burned all of his letters. Our baby girl didn't deserve to be second to no one, especially not a revolting heathen like you. You would have been nothing but a horrid influence. I—"

The laughter that escapes my body is high-pitched and honestly quite frightening. Once it's loose, I can't control it. It consumes my insides, and I double over, mirth spilling with abandon.

"See? That's exactly what I mean. You are nothing but a waste of space. Here you stand by your father's grave, and you—"

"Look, lady," Ty's voice says above me, though my laughter is still booming. "I think it's time you left." The authority in his voice sends a shiver down my spine. I definitely wouldn't ever want to get on Tyler Boston's bad side. He gently extracts himself from my grasp and steps around me, putting himself between my step mom and me.

"Who in God's name do you think you are? It's her that needs to go!"

Tyler turns to me. "I'll be right back." He crosses the short distance in two strides, then leans in and whispers something to the deranged woman. Her eyes widen almost comically, but her mouth clamps shut. In my half-crazed state of mind, I think of what she would look like as a cartoon at this exact moment. Smoke would gush from her ears, and a deep red color would crawl its way up her neck to her face. She would have a thought bubble with grawlix depicting the curses she's thinking. That line of thinking only triggers another round of giggles, and I find it hard to stay upright now that Ty isn't beside me.

With one final hate-filled glare she turns and leaves without a backward glance.

Tyler walks back to me, sorrow filling his eyes.

"He wrote me," I whisper once my heaving body has calmed. "He wrote me, Ty." He sighs deeply, then wraps an arm around me and guides me back to the car. I steal one final look at the grave behind me.

"Goodbye, Dad."

Chapter 25

Jace

I'm hunting, stalking my prey as I sit in the corner of the strip club, sipping water to keep my head clear. My eyes see everything and nothing all at the same time. The trio of strippers to my left pass out small baggies to various patrons. Drugs.

The man three booths down from mine is getting just what he paid for. Sex.

The middle-aged man with salt-and-pepper hair directly across from me is who I've come for. He likes 'em young. Too young. I wonder if the girl on his lap even actually works here. There's no way she's eighteen. As I watch him, my resolve solidifies. This despicable excuse of a human is going to get everything he has coming to him. The fact that I'm going to be the one to deliver that fate sends a calming surge through my veins. All I have to do is wait and pretend to be interested in the birds that float by. Mostly, I've been handing them cash and telling them to get the fuck away from me. One girl looks a little nervous, first night maybe, so I tell her she can sit at my table for a while. I rebuff all her whispered offers, all the while keeping the man, the pedo, in my peripheral. When he gets up, I slip the frightened girl another wad of cash and follow him out the back.

Cool metal shifts against my back with each step. The man pushes open the alley door and walks out, his boots thudding on the pavement.

I would like to believe he's shit at his job, that he has no idea he's being followed, but after the way he left his girl, not even taking her with him, I know he's on high alert. As I step out into the darkened alleyway, I'm prepared for the blow that comes at me. I duck, and the clank of a metal pipe hitting the brick wall echoes behind me. I turn quickly, throwing my fists at the pillock of a man. My final hook knocks him off his feet. Towering over him, I pull the gun from the waistband of my jeans. Right as I take aim, a sharp pain collides with my knee.

I buckle under my own weight and drop the gun. It skitters across the ground with a sickening metallic scrape. I try to roll, but the man is on top of me, fists hammering into my face. I shrimp away and cover my face, creating enough space to pull him into my guard. Stupidly he reaches for my neck, and as he does, I pivot my hips and wrap my hands around his arm. The bone cracks under me as I thrust my back upward with all my strength.

I hear screams of pain and then a voice I thought I wouldn't hear again.

I look up and there she is.

No.

No, no, no!

What the fuck is she doing here, now? I want to be angry. I want to yell, to tell her to leave, but I freeze. A knee collides with my eye socket, making my vision go dark for a second. When I come to, I'm staring down the barrel of a loaded gun.

"You went down fucking easy for having the reputation you do. Say good night, mother-fucker!"

Blood sprays onto my face, and horrible flashbacks stun me for a moment—until I hear crying. Jumping to my feet, I see the man on the ground, groaning and holding his stomach as blood pools around him.

Lexi is still aiming the gun at him. My gun. Her hands tremble violently. I lift the man's gun from the ground and rush toward her. Gently placing my hand over hers, I pull the gun from her vice-like grip.

"I killed him—I killed him. He was going to kill you, so I killed him..." Her voice is haunting, and it rips right through my chest.

No—no, no! FUCK!

"Hey, hey, hey." I take her face into my hands, forcing her to look away from the bastard. "No...no you didn't."

"Yes! Yes, I did I shot him. I—I..." Not able to

handle the pain and torment in her eyes, I turn, firing three rounds into the man. He instantly stops moving.

"No, look, I killed him, okay? Not you. Me," I say, not thinking that it will immediately cause her to look at a dead man. She starts to look, but I pull her face into my hands, again locking eyes with her. "I killed him," I say in a calm tone, but a wetness builds behind my eyes the whole time. "Okay?"

Her bewitching cerulean eyes see me and all my dark fucking glory. She knows. My chest grows tight, and all I want to do is take her pain away. I grit my teeth as I stare into her eyes, fear consuming me so completely I cannot breathe.

Tears leave trails down her beautiful face as she nods. Pulling her into my chest, I squeeze and take a deep breath. Then I begin to walk her away but end up rounding on Tyler and Diah with my gun as they burst out of the back door of the club. Tyler's eyes flash to the body and back. His shoulders visibly slouch, and he cuts his eyes to me.

"Lexi, are you okay?" he asks, and the pain thickens. He blames me, just as he should.

She nods, and another hole burns into my heart. I replace my gun and continue walking Lexi away from the scene behind us, trying not to be consumed with thoughts of what's to come.

Chapter 26

Lexi

In the shower I try to rid myself of the images, but no matter how much I try, the man's pockmarked face still looks down on Jace, ready to end his life, exactly like he ended my father's. When I saw the gun on the ground, I didn't even think. I simply reacted. It wasn't until I saw the blood, heard his moaning, and the copper smell hit me like a brick wall that I began to melt down. My hands are still shaking, a cold sensation making my fingertips numb. Jace watches me with hooded eyes as he pushes the washcloth over my body, cleaning away the blood he smeared on me when he held me as we drove back to the hotel.

"Lexi." His voice is thick, yet steady. It breathes life back into me, pulling me from my self-made prison.

I blink up at him, seeing the blood splattered across his face. Breathing deep, I take the rag from him and began wiping it away. The water turns pink as we wash away the evidence.

No matter how crazy, dangerous and wrong Jace's past was he is actively trying to forge a different path. Clearly feeling like the Marines were his only option, he hid the knowledge from anyone who threatened to take away his chance at leaving this life behind. I could easily see how I would unknowingly hold him back. I understood that he didn't choose the biker title, that he was born into it. I understood his desperation to leave it. I even understood the justice he wanted to lay at my feet, in honor of my father. What I didn't understand was why it was hurting so terribly bad and there wasn't a damn thing I could do about it. I feel our time together slipping away and it all seems obsolete.

I lie on the bed, wrapped in nothing but a robe, while Jace gives Tyler the bag containing our clothes.

Tyler watches me from the doorway.

"Get rid of it," I hear Jace say. "And find something for her to wear." Ty leaves, and the bed behind me dips. His hands are gentle as they pull me back into him. His warmth tries its hardest to chase away my chill. I turn into him, so many questions on my lips, but as my eyes search his, the questions dissipate in the air between us.

"I...I don't..." He closes his eyes and inhales unsteadily. "I am so sorry for everything."

In that moment, I don't want to talk. I don't want to hear his apologies. I don't want to think about any of it. I simply want to forget, even if it only lasts a little while. Slowly, I close the space between us. At first his lips are stiff and unresponsive. Then all at once, he's alive, kissing me as though it will be out last time together.

∞∞∞

The next day I know we have to part ways. I know there's no way he can stay, not now that a man is dead, regardless of who killed him. I still don't know his name, the man I killed. Jace has no choice but to continue with his path into the Marines, and I feel like it's all my fault.

When he draws me into his arms one final time, I want to tell him not to go, that we can run away together, go to a different country and live our lives together. My insides feel as though I've been poisoned. Everything hurts. Every iota of my being is trying to reject the reality that's unfolding. I want to kiss him again. I want...I want to tell him that I love him and that I will wait for him for as long as it takes. Instead, I just hold him a little tighter.

The emotions in his eyes mimic my own, and some of the poison fades. He pulls away too quickly, and the oxygen is sucked from my lungs. He leaves me with no goodbye kiss, no farewell, nothing until he opens the car door. As he begins to climb inside he pauses and looks back at me.

His lips part in a beautiful smile before he winks. My breath is knocked back into me, and I fall to my knees. When the tears clear, he's gone.

Thank you Mike, for giving me the inspiration and experience to write this beautiful love story. Without you it would've been awfully boring.

About The Author

Randie Craft was raised solely by her adoptive mother after her adoptive parents divorced, at the age of eight. She was a competitive female amateur M.M.A fighter. Now she focuses more on the art of Brazilian Jiu-Jitsu, and her innate desire to become an author and renowned artist. She is a mother of two children and a wife of nine years. Her son and husband both have Autism and sensory disorders. The past few years have been the hardest of her life so far; her mother was taken by cancer. Still she knows there is beauty, hope and love in the world, however, because of the stories she has read and the art that has inspired her throughout life.

https://www.facebook.com/RandieArtist

Made in the USA
Middletown, DE
16 August 2022

70590502R00106